# IMPASSIVE

*An indebted publisher meets his death in Kirkstall Abbey*

## RAY CLARK

THE
BOOK
FOLKS

Published by The Book Folks

London, 2021

© Ray Clark

This book is a work of fiction. Names, characters, businesses, organizations, places and events are either the product of the author's imagination or are used fictitiously. Any resemblance to actual persons, living or dead, events or locales is entirely coincidental.

All rights reserved. No part of this publication may be reproduced, stored in retrieval system, copied in any form or by any means, electronic, mechanical, photocopying, recording or otherwise transmitted without written permission from the publisher.

ISBN  978-1-913516-14-7

www.thebookfolks.com

*"If all mankind minus one, were of one opinion, and only one person were of the contrary opinion, mankind would be no more justified in silencing that one person, than he, if he had the power, would be justified in silencing mankind."*

John Stuart Mill

# Chapter One

As midnight approached, Ronnie Robinson realised he had been skulking around Kirkstall Abbey for more than an hour, dressed in only a raincoat, which wasn't helping, as the weather was now starting to turn: the wind had dropped, the sky was clear, and the inevitable frost was starting to cling to his bones.

But he was desperate for some action.

He adjusted his face mask; a tight red number, which had oval white lines outlining the face, and then crossing left to right: with holes for the eyes, nose and mouth.

Kirkstall was a world away from Farnley, where he lived, but he figured he'd pushed his luck a little too far on that patch. The last time he'd nearly been caught; which shows you how a night in the pub and a skinful of ale altered one's perception of things – except the ugly mob that had taken chase. Luckily for him it had been close to home.

But to do what he had in mind, it was adrenaline you needed, and tonight he had it in spades.

Ronnie squinted in the direction of his watch and kept moving his wrist around to reflect what little light he had.

"Should have gone to fucking Specsavers," he moaned.

Then he heard female voices.

Ronnie ducked and glanced around. He was thirty or forty yards from the A65 with the ruined building on his left. Traffic was light to non-existent and he saw no one walking in either direction.

1

Adrenaline was pumping now. He'd popped a pill about twenty to thirty minutes back and now he had a boner like the Eiffel Tower. One last check around and Ronnie scuttled forward in the direction of the voices, walking like he had three legs.

He covered the ground quite quickly. At the end of the building he slipped left, past the entrance guarded by the iron gate. He slinked further into the shadows, leaning against a low stone wall.

The voices grew nearer but he still couldn't see anyone. Mind you, he couldn't see his fucking watch and that had only been a matter of inches away. You'd think he'd have a better chance of seeing two fully-grown humans.

He slithered closer to the side of the building, pressing his scrawny body into a darkened recess. It was definitely two women. They were rattling on about shopping and other crap.

Ronnie heard a dog bark. He rolled his eyes. That could be a problem.

His breathing grew more erratic, and he was becoming light-headed. Glancing in all directions, he still couldn't see anyone else approaching. He wished to God they would hurry up.

His wish was suddenly granted. One of them laughed loudly and he realised they were much closer than he had thought. A few more steps and they were his.

As the women drew level he noticed one was blonde, the other was dark-haired. Both were dressed in thick coats and jeans and wearing wellington boots. They were holding hands, paying little attention to anyone other than themselves.

As quick as a flash, Ronnie stepped out of the shadows with his raincoat open and his arms extended – everything on show.

"What about this, then, girls, how's about a bit of real man action?"

They both stopped dead, stared in his direction and suddenly burst out laughing.

That was not the reaction Ronnie was expecting.

The dog suddenly started barking and pulling at the lead.

"If that's all you've got, mate, I wouldn't bother," shouted the blonde, a little overweight with a face like a blind cobbler's thumb.

The dark-haired one brought her hand to her mouth. "I've seen bigger toothpicks."

Further laughter ensued. The dog was one of those snappy little shits with plenty of bottle so it was still straining at the lead.

Ronnie was in trouble. He had no idea how to react to the situation. It had never happened before.

"Get home, you pathetic lump of shite," shouted the blonde.

"Yeah, come back when you've really got something to show us."

If the laughing and the abuse were unexpected, their next move was totally against the rules.

The blonde bent down and picked up a rock, launching it in his direction.

Ronnie put his left arm up and moved to the right, which didn't do him any favours because the rock hit his right shoulder and knocked him off balance.

She then let the dog go, which charged over like a cruise missile, sinking its teeth into Ronnie's right ankle.

Ronnie screeched and tried to push the dog off, but it wasn't having any of it.

The women laughed even more, almost doubling up hysterically.

"Get off, you bastard," shouted Ronnie. That didn't help because the dog sensed the aggression and dug in harder, and actually tried to pull him back to its owners.

Ronnie managed to struggle to his feet, where another rock hit him square in the face.

If the laughter and the abuse and the dog biting him was bad, what happened next almost blew his mind; it almost blew all of their minds.

Two incredibly bright flashes of white light lit up the inside of the derelict building.

"Oh, fuck," shouted Ronnie, trying to close the raincoat.

The women stopped laughing. The dog let go, whined and scurried back to them, when another bright flash of light enveloped the area.

"What the bloody hell was that?" shouted the blonde.

"Search me," said the one with dark hair, "but I'm not hanging around to find out. Come on."

The blonde scooped the dog into her arms and the pair of them ran towards the A65.

Ronnie wasn't stopping either. He quickly turned and lurched forward, straight into the low stone wall with his right knee. The pain was so sharp and so severe that his legs buckled.

"Jesus," he shouted, rubbing his knee and squinting into the darkness. "Who the fuck put that there?"

Unwilling to waste any further time, he jumped to his feet, tied the raincoat and hobbled off as quickly as he could, as if auditioning for the part of Quasimodo; he'd have passed with flying colours.

The night was ruined.

As he ran around the front of the building and to his right he was suddenly enveloped in another flash of blinding light, which lit up the entire interior.

Ronnie ducked and shielded his face with his hands. What the fuck was going on? Had he been caught on some stupid reality TV show: *I'm a Fucking Perv, Get Me Out of Here?*

Trussed up like a Bernard Matthews turkey he'd pressed himself into the wall of the building, listening closely, but he couldn't hear anything.

He removed his hands from his face and glanced up at the huge arch shaped opening, which could at one time have been a window. Below it was a ledge he could probably stand on.

Slowly and carefully he raised himself up, dashed across to the ledge, stood on the top and peered over the sill, into the building.

Another blinding flash of light scorched his eyeballs. But he saw enough to realise that hanging around was the last thing he should do.

Ronnie turned and ran.

He wasn't having any of that.


# Chapter Two


*Wednesday: 06.15 hrs*

Adi Giles pulled his battered VW camper van to a shuddering stop in the abbey visitor's centre. He switched it off and jumped out. The poor old thing needed a service. He'd recently had a health check done at one of the garages and they'd found all sorts wrong with it. Where he was going to find the money to pay for it all he had no idea.

Closing and locking the door he glanced across the road at the abbey. It was early morning, late March. The building was enshrouded by mist. The photos would be perfect. He'd spent most of the previous day worrying about that as well. *Would the conditions be right? Would there be a ground mist? Had he remembered to charge the batteries in his camera equipment?*

No real worries on that score because he had the ancient but reliable 35mm with him as well. He enjoyed old-fashioned photography, particularly the art of developing.

Adi blew into his hands and opened the back of the vehicle, pulling out the two shoulder bags he had brought with him. He closed the door, locked the vehicle, picked up the bags and set off across the A65 to the ancient monument.

Halfway across the road his mind went into overdrive as he started to worry about the pending court case, if it went that far. Adi still couldn't believe the publisher had ripped him off. It was so blatantly obvious that they had gone out and taken their own photographs, with slight differences to be able to pass them off as their own: altered the description under the pictures and passed the whole book off as theirs.

Well, he wasn't having any of that. He'd spoken to a solicitor and the Society of Authors, neither of which gave him any really encouraging advice, but he still felt he had to do something. That had caused him three months of sleepless nights and worry-filled days.

Entering the grounds, first light was beginning to show. Hopefully, he would finish up with some great snaps.

Adi stopped and quickly checked his phone, hoping to see a message from Freddie. Nothing had appeared, which caused him to worry about that. Freddie, his partner of three years, worked as a porter in a seedy hotel in a seedy part of Leeds. He worked nights, which took him through to around eight in the morning. It was a dreadful place with all sorts of drug deals going down. Freddie then slept most of the day and started work again in the early evening, so they saw very little of each other.

Putting his phone back in his pocket, Adi noticed a bench seat near the abbey and flopped onto it. He felt completely exhausted. Adi was confused because he felt sure he *had* slept right through last night. He couldn't remember waking to go to the toilet, or for any other reason, so why the hell was he so tired?

There was perhaps something wrong with him. He had not been to the doctor for years, even though he knew you were supposed to go for a check-up at least once a year. It could be something serious, like cancer. Or maybe a blood-related problem; perhaps even a brain tumour. He didn't like the sound of that, and sticking your head in the sand forever wouldn't help. But he wasn't keen on doctors either.

Adi stood up and banished the thoughts from his mind. Whatever it was, it wasn't a regular occurrence. Most days he felt okay. He ate well all the time. Being a vegan meant he wasn't shovelling garbage into his system, so it couldn't be anything to do with that.

He picked up his camera equipment. If he didn't make a move and shoot something soon, the whole thing would be a waste of time. Then he would have lost a complete day, and plenty of money, leaving him with something else to worry about.

He hoisted the first bag over his shoulder. When he tried to do the same with the other, the strap came loose, and the bag dropped and hit the ground. Some of the equipment rolled out.

"Oh, for God's sake," muttered Adi.

Pushing it all back in, he tightened the strap and picked it up. Glancing at the abbey he decided he would start inside the ruined cloister building, so he made his way around to the right side.

He glanced around the grounds. It was very quiet, not even a dog walker. Staring back at the road he saw very little traffic. Good. No interruptions meant he could settle down to do some work.

Adi set off quickly, reaching the tall iron gates leading into the grounds. He pushed open one of them, and it squeaked, setting his nerves on edge and causing him to grind his teeth.

Squeezing through he pulled his phone out of his pocket – still no message from Freddie. A short text to say he was okay was all it would take to set Adi's mind at rest.

Walking forward, he suddenly thought of what he had to do once he'd finished his assignment. The photos would need developing, and the digital ones uploading. Middle of the week meant a top-up shop. The place needed cleaning and he couldn't expect Freddie to do it because he worked all night, and Adi worked for himself so technically he had more time. *What time?* He never seemed to have any. Christ, it never ended.

He quickly put his phone away and glanced upwards, having nearly reached the end of the abbey building.

Adi froze completely.

"Oh my good God!"

# Chapter Three

Stewart Gardener had risen early and was now in the garage, raring to go. The fire-damaged speakers were nicely warmed up, the hi-fi currently playing *Sarah* by Fleetwood Mac, which he felt was a rather fitting tribute – finally. His mind was clear, there were no pending cases requiring his attention.

He was staring at his pride and joy when a noise from behind caught his attention. His father, Malcolm, walked through the open door carrying a tray with three teas, three bacon sandwiches, and a bottle of ketchup. Chris, his son, close behind.

"What are you trying to do to me?" asked Gardener, staring at the sandwiches.

"Thought we'd come and see what all the racket was about," said Malcolm.

"As if you couldn't guess." Gardener glanced at Chris and then his father. "Who got *him* up?"

"Nobody," replied Chris with an expression that informed his father he was quite put out by the remark.

"I doubt if he's even been to bed, yet," said Malcolm.

"Come on, Dad, you must remember what it was like to be young," said Chris. "Or maybe not, that is quite some time back."

"You cheeky bugger," said Gardener, feinting with his left. Chris ducked but Gardener was too quick, grabbing him in the type of hug where they wrestled around, laughing and joking. Eventually Gardener let go and Chris hugged him properly, before stepping back.

"I wouldn't miss today for the world," said his son.

"Neither of us would," said Malcolm, placing the tray on a bench. "Come on, get these while they're still warm."

In the last year and a half, Chris had filled out a lot. He'd shot up and was a few inches short of Gardener's height. He'd added a bit of weight, but he worked out, so it wasn't fat. His hair was overdue for a cut, but Gardener had long since given up the ghost on that discussion. He was more than pleased that, because there were only three of them in the family, they had remained close and blended very well.

"I'm just pleased that all *three* of us have this day to celebrate," said Malcolm.

"What do you mean?" asked Gardener, reaching for his sandwich, and the ketchup.

"The hospital, or have you conveniently forgotten about it?"

Gardener hadn't; he knew his father had a point. He strolled toward the garage door, breathing in the fresh morning air, realising how good life actually was, how lucky he *was* to be alive. Three months previous, he had been in a hospital bed for a week after some maniac had pumped him full of Secobarbital. The allergic reaction lasted three days, and he spent another two recovering with a rather nice blonde nurse at his beck and call.

"That was a while back," replied Gardener, tuning back in, playing it down. "I'm fine now."

"It was still a worrying time for us two."

"It was just a bit of a reaction, Dad. I was never in any real danger."

"We didn't know that. It could have gone either way. I keep telling you how dangerous your job is, maybe now you'll finally believe me."

"Someone has to do it."

"Doesn't make it any easier. And why you?"

"Why not me?" replied Gardener.

"That's not an answer. I think it's time you started concentrating on what you have, taking things easy? We have a nice house, close family. We all do all right. Give it up, concentrate on your bike, or at least reduce your hours."

"Come on," said Gardener, "have you ever heard of a part-time detective? No way would that work; clocking off in the middle of a murder case because it's a zero-hours contract and I've worked my designated time. Briggs would love that."

"It would work if you were sitting at a desk."

"Out of the question, Dad. I'm not a desk jockey," Gardener bit back. "You can't wrap me in cotton wool. Besides, it wouldn't pay the bills."

"I have some money put by."

Gardener winced. "I think we've been here before, Dad. Anyway, I like my job. It's what gets me up in a morning, and what keeps me going throughout the day. You never know what's going to land in your inbox. Every murder is something different. And it's coming home after a long hard day, or week, as the case may be, and seeing you guys waiting for me." He suddenly changed tactics in an effort to lighten the mood. "Anyway, if I gave up the job, I know one thing we couldn't afford."

"Go on," said Malcolm, staring at his butty, perhaps wondering where to start.

"*His* food bill," replied Gardener, pointing at Chris.

All three laughed.

"Leave me out of it," said Chris, staring at the bike, a 1959 T120 Triumph Bonneville, in pristine condition and ready for action.

Gardener's mind was suddenly cast back to the fateful night in Leeds when his wife had been shot and killed.

The Bonneville was the last thing Sarah had bought him, the present she had referred to when she'd said she had employed the help of his father. Sarah knew Gardener had wanted a Triumph Bonneville for as long as he could remember. He'd never found the right one, or the right time to buy one.

His father discovered it in a breaker's yard when he had been searching for spare parts for a friend. The owner hadn't even known it was there. Malcolm told Sarah. She made an offer.

His father picked up the bike that fateful afternoon, waiting until they had gone out before smuggling it into the garage. Sarah knew Gardener would have devoted his entire life to the well-being of the bike.

And boy had it seen better days: when purchased, the tyres were bald, the exhaust rusty, hanging off; the seat chewed by rats. The badge on the fuel tank had been missing, the tank itself worn down to bare metal. There was no front number plate. The headlamp was smashed. The list was endless.

"Nervous?" his father asked.

"A little."

"It'll pass."

The fully restored machine sparkled. Chris had spent most of the previous day polishing it. The whole thing had been lifted from the home-made frame his father had concocted for the restoration, and now stood on its own stand.

Everything had been painstakingly checked and repaired or replaced, and the bike now had a new King and Queen seat which had 3D Net inserts to ensure optimum comfort for both rider and passenger, with button detailing and an embroidered Triumph wordmark. The reviews said that it was extremely comfortable with an added bonus of extra seat height for the passenger.

"I take it you haven't fired it up, yet?" asked Malcolm, passing over a sandwich and a mug of tea to Chris, whose first bite demolished a quarter of it immediately.

"No," said Gardener.

"What are you waiting for?"

"I don't know. I want to start it but I don't. I have a million questions running through my head: *will* it start? What if something's wrong? What will it drive like?"

"You won't be the first. We all feel like that after a big restoration like this one," said Malcolm. "But you'll have to start it sometime."

"You know, it's strange, they do say you should never meet your idols. I have wanted one of these for as long as I can remember, but what if it's not the bike I thought it would be, or hoped for?"

"I don't think there's any danger of that," Malcolm replied.

"Do you want *me* to do it, Dad?" asked Chris, sandwich totally finished with only crumbs remaining on the garage floor.

Gardener appreciated the offer but it had to be him. He placed his empty plate on the bench. Walking forward heightened his tension. He gripped the handlebars, cocked a leg over and levered out the kick-start.

His mobile rang.

Gardener glanced at it. The number belonged to Millgarth. At such an early hour, it could only be the desk sergeant with bad news.

Gardener stepped off the bike, almost relieved.

# Chapter Four

DI Stewart Gardener and DS Sean Reilly were standing in the grounds of the abbey within thirty minutes of the call-out. They flashed their warrant cards to the PC standing guard, signed the scene log, suited and booted, donned fresh gloves, and stepped through the tall metal gate leading into the ruined church.

Gardener would readily admit that he didn't know much about the place other than it was in a public park on the north bank of the River Aire, founded c.1152. It was disestablished during the Dissolution of the Monasteries under Henry VIII.

He glanced around. The church was of the Cistercian type with a short chancel, and transepts, with three eastward chapels to each, divided by solid walls. The building was plain, the windows unornamented, and the nave had no triforium. The cloister to the south occupied the whole length of the nave with a gate at the end, with stone columns running the entire length. At the presbytery end was a huge, pointed arch that had probably been home to a window. Down the middle was a stone path with grass either side. They might be lucky with evidence.

He remembered that the abbey was also used for a live BBC Three event, *Frankenstein's Wedding... Live in Leeds* in 2011, and in the same year, the Kaiser Chiefs played two concerts at the abbey to a maximum audience of 10,000 on each day.

But he never had it down as the scene of a public hanging.

"This *is* interesting," said Reilly.

Gardener reached the presbytery end and stared upwards. He had no idea how tall the building was but the rope from which the man was hanging had been tied around a beam in the roof – and that was high.

"How the hell did he get here?" Gardener asked.

On first glance, the dead man was probably mid-sixties. His complexion was anaemic but under the circumstances that could be expected; balding, with clumps of brown hair down the side. His skin texture was rough. He was skeletally thin and not very tall, dressed in a powder blue suit with a white shirt, open at the neck – no tie. There were dark stains around the trouser legs, which resembled mud.

Reilly studied the man's shoes. "Good quality leather. They're not cheap."

Gardener was examining the man's wrist. "Neither is the gold watch. I'm not an expert but I know enough to know that an Omega is a make worth having."

Gardener wondered who he was and what he did for a living. He checked the man's pockets but they were all empty, which meant no ID. Reilly walked around the back of the corpse.

"I think we can rule out suicide."

"It's highly unlikely," replied Gardener, "given the fact that we can't see any means of getting himself up there, and there doesn't appear to be a note."

"I was thinking more the fact of how clean he is."

Gardener glanced at Reilly, and immediately cottoned on to what he was talking about. He, too, checked the back of the corpse. He'd seen enough suicides at the end of a rope in his time to know that whilst you're struggling, you always soil yourself.

"But even if it's murder, Sean, it begs the question, how did he end up here? Who managed to get the rope all the way up there – and how? Whoever did this, they were very careful."

Reilly stared at the ground and then at the arched window opening. "Any ladders could have been hoisted through there."

Gardener also studied the ground. Below the corpse it was concrete, which was unlikely to reveal much.

"There had to be more than one of them," suggested Reilly, "but I don't see any signs of a struggle. If he knew what was coming, you'd have expected him to put up a fight."

"Unless he was sedated," pointed out Gardener.

"Maybe," said Reilly.

"Or already dead," Gardener added.

"So why hang him?"

"There'll be a reason."

Gardener reached and took a pulse purely as a matter of habit. The man was definitely deceased, which meant they had all the time in the world to play around with the scene. He wasn't going anywhere, and the roof was a natural covering, so he didn't really need to worry about the weather.

Reilly peered more closely at the head and neck of the victim. "You could be right about him already being dead, boss. The rope is under the chin and right up behind the ears, but his throat is marked. I'm sure Dr Death will tell us, when he shows up."

"Don't you go winding him up," said Gardener.

"As if."

Gardener reached into his jacket pocket for his mobile and called the desk sergeant at Millgarth. He asked for his team: the Home Office pathologist, a team of SOCOs; and PolSA for a fingertip search. He also wanted tents, and though he had also considered ruling it out, he asked for a call to be put into the Met Office to check weather conditions.

Once finished he turned to his partner.

"We need to treat the hanging and surrounding area as a standard murder scene. I don't want to move the body unless I have to. Once we do that, we've lost the whole thing. We'll drop a cordon around it, and we'll cover the building."

"Build the tent around it, you mean?"

"More or less," said Gardener.

"They're gonna love you for that."

"I was just thinking that. We'll need to photograph it all and examine the approach/regress; make sure we don't miss any footprints or anything else that might be important."

Reilly made notes for when the team arrived, before adding, "We'll need Fitz to check if there are any defence marks on the body."

"We'd better get the clothes checked for fibre taping, look for any third-party DNA on the cuffs and the collar," said Gardener. "There's no way this guy did it to himself."

"Another question we need to answer," said Reilly. "Was it done here?"

Gardener glanced at the gate and the PC standing guard, and then at his watch. "I wonder what sort of a window we're looking at. When and where was he killed; when was he brought here?"

"I've no idea," said Reilly, "but if it was during the wee hours, someone would have needed a lot of light. That would surely have attracted someone's attention."

"You'd have thought so," said Gardener. "Imagine driving your car along the A65 around midnight and seeing this place light up from the inside. Would have looked pretty supernatural."

"The phone lines should have been red-hot."

"Instead we have one phone call at around six o'clock this morning. Talking of which, while we wait for the team to arrive, maybe we should go and speak to the man who found him."

# Chapter Five

He was sitting on a bench, wrapped in a blanket, shaking and obviously worrying. The only thing Gardener knew about him was his name, which the PC attending the scene had provided.

Adrian Giles glanced up as they approached. He smiled, but it certainly wasn't a joyous expression.

Gardener nodded and took a space on the bench next to him. Reilly sat opposite on a slab of concrete, with his notebook at the ready.

Gardener liked what he saw at first glance because the man had a homely quality about him – though he must have been at the back of the queue when good looks were handed out. His face had the shape of a walnut; all rugged and bumpy in a Sid James sort of way: a bit like a well-kept grave, with spiky blond hair that had been gelled and arranged to hide some of the developing baldness. His dress sense was a little flamboyant: pink shirt and black leather trousers.

"Mr Giles?" questioned Gardener, displaying his warrant card. "Detective Inspector Stewart Gardener and Detective Sergeant Sean Reilly of the West Yorkshire Major Investigation Team."

He nodded. "I'm sorry, I'm not sure how much use I'll be." He was very softly spoken and Gardener had to strain to hear him.

"You'd be surprised, Mr Giles. If you're up for a few questions we'd really appreciate it."

Giles nodded again.

"Would you like a strong, sweet tea?" Gardener asked, noticing a van across at the visitor's centre.

"A stiff *G & T* might hit the mark sooner."

"That could be a problem, son," said Reilly, "especially at this time of the morning."

Giles smiled. "Sorry, I thought a bit of levity might help."

"I find it usually does," said Reilly.

"Can we start with some personal stuff, Mr Giles? I know your name so perhaps you can let me have you full address, where you work, and what brought you here so early this morning?"

Giles told him that home was a moderate three-bedroom semi in Horsforth, though one of them was a darkroom for developing photos, which he went on to explain was his profession.

"You're a photographer," said Gardener. "Self-employed?"

"Yes."

"Do you specialise in anything?"

"This stuff," said Giles, pointing to the abbey.

"Can you elaborate a little?"

"I've always loved photography, officer," replied Giles, as if it was somehow illegal. "I enjoy photographing old abbeys and listed buildings with character. And then I like to research any dark connections to them, which I can use with my photos to add a little history."

"You into that sort of stuff, then?" asked Reilly.

"Only in photos," said Giles. "God knows why, most anything else usually frightens me rigid. I can't watch that *Paranormal Caught on Camera* that Freddie likes to watch. It freaks me out. I go to bed imagining all sorts; that whatever I've just seen is in the house with me."

"Guess you won't be sleeping much tonight, then," offered Reilly.

"I'll say. It's not every day you find someone you know at the end of a rope."

"You know him?" asked Gardener, glancing at his partner.

"Oh, God," cried Giles, bringing his hands to his face. "This is just awful."

Gardener allowed him a minute and then asked if he could take him through his movements from leaving the house to finding the corpse.

Giles related it all while Reilly took notes. Gardener stopped him now and again for a couple of reasons; firstly, in an effort to slow him down because no one living could write that fast, and secondly, to make sure he didn't miss out any details.

Gardener glanced over at the visitor's centre. "Are any of those vehicles yours?"

"The battered camper van."

"Were there any vehicles parked there when you arrived that have since gone?"

Giles turned and studied the scene. "No, the blue one and the silver one were there. The black one next to mine wasn't."

"That's ours," said Reilly.

"When you arrived, did you see anyone else around?"

Giles shook his head. "Not that I can recall. It was probably a bit early for most people."

"No suspicious looking people milling around?" asked Reilly.

"Like someone struggling with a big pair of ladders strapped to his back, you mean?" Giles started to laugh and then stopped suddenly. "Oh, God, that's not really very funny, is it? I'm so sorry, it's just nerves."

Gardener could accept that. Adi Giles definitely appeared that sort.

"Okay, so no people around. Once you entered the grounds, which end of the abbey did you go to?"

"That end," he pointed, "the one with the gate entry."

"And there was still no one around at that point?"

"No."

"So when you eventually found the deceased, you didn't touch anything?"

"No. God, no," said Giles, horrified. "I got my stuff together and cleared out as fast as I could. That time of the morning you've no idea who's hanging around in the shadows. Whoever did that to him might still have been here. I didn't feel safe. I came straight out. Touched nothing. I've seen enough police programs to know better."

Gardener wondered if he was actually going to stop talking. When he finally did, Gardener asked him the name of the dead man.

Giles hesitated and peered up to the sky. His eyes were watering slightly but he managed to compose himself.

"His name is Max Knowles."

"How do you know him, Mr Giles?"

"He's a publisher."

"Is he local?"

"He has an office in the Kirkgate Chambers."

That rang a bell with Gardener. He suddenly remembered a solicitor by the name of Wilfred Ronson, a right old soak who made a living representing the dregs of society. Still, he wouldn't be doing that again. Gardener watched the man drop dead last year on a railway station, right before his eyes.

Giles continued, quickly, "Well, it's not actually Kirkgate Chambers." He stared at Gardener. "Do you know Kirkgate in Leeds?"

Gardener nodded.

"Well, Kirkgate Chambers is to the left of the entrance for the City Market. His office is to the right. It's a chamber but I'm not sure what they call it. The building is about four storeys high, with a business on each floor. It's a right dump. They're on the top floor."

"They?" questioned Reilly.

Giles nodded. "He runs it with his brother, Cyril. Be careful with him, he's like a Rottweiler with a hangover."

"Don't worry, we have an antidote for people like him," said Gardener, glancing at his partner.

"Cyril's that tight, the only way to get a warm drink out of him is to stick your fingers down his throat."

Reilly laughed at the comment. "We might give that a go."

"So how do you know Cyril and Max Knowles, Mr Giles?"

"Our paths have crossed. Everybody in that game seems to know everybody else. Especially publishers: if at first you don't succeed and all that. We all send our work out to all of them."

"Do they specialise in the type of book you produce?"

Giles hesitated before answering. "Not really, they're more into autobiographies. Mainly local people, of the sporting variety."

"You mentioned someone called Freddie earlier."

Giles smiled and nodded. "He's my boyfriend, partner, whatever you want to call it. The term keeps changing nowadays. Some of them are not very nice."

"What does he do, Mr Giles?"

"Works for probably one of the seediest hotels in Leeds. Bloody awful place in Ruffin Street. The Ruffin, that's what it's called. All sorts going down. He's a night porter."

"I imagine you don't see much of each other."

"Not a lot."

"Was he working last night?"

Giles suddenly checked his phone. "Yes. I worry about him, that's why I checked my phone."

"If he works in Ruffin Street, I'm worried about him," said Reilly, "and I don't even know him."

Gardener changed topics. "To come back to the publisher, do the brothers run it by themselves, or do they have staff?"

"They have a secretary called Vera Purdy. She's reasonably mild compared to them two."

"Was Max like his brother?"

"Not far off, but a lot more civil. He'd call you behind your back, whereas Cyril will do it to your face."

"What's the name of the business?"

"Kirkstall House Publishing."

"When was the last time you saw either of them?"

Giles stared vacantly at the abbey. "I can't really remember. Perhaps a month or six weeks back, to be honest. There was something going on in one of the galleries in Leeds. They were there, drinking the place dry."

Heavy drinkers, thought Gardener. He was keen to delve into the business to see how well it was doing, but he was certainly very pleased with the information he had received from Adi Giles. As he couldn't think of anything further to ask, he offered Giles a card and said they would more than likely be in touch again, but if he remembered anything else to call Gardener directly; and then asked if he needed transport home.

"No, no, I'm fine, officer. I think I'll sit here a bit longer if that's okay."

"It's fine by us, son, but just keep away from the cordoned area," said Reilly. "Are you sure you wouldn't like that drink?"

Giles shook his head. "I'm not sure I could keep anything down this morning."

Gardener noticed members of his team arriving and parking up in the visitor's centre. The Home Office pathologist had also made it to the abbey.

As the two officers walked away from Giles, Gardener turned back. "It may sound an odd question, but you didn't actually take any photos yourself, did you?"

"Are you kidding," said Giles. "I was out of there the second I saw what had happened."

Gardener nodded and set off in the direction of the presbytery end, the one with the arched window. As they reached it, he squatted down and checked the ground.

"What do you think, Sean, about our Mr Giles?"

"He seems harmless enough. Certainly shaken up by it all."

"I wondered if Laura knows him, being in a similar line of business."

"I'm not sure," said Reilly. Laura was his wife. "I'll ask her when I get home. I certainly haven't heard of him."

Gardener turned his attention to the ground. "Looks like there's a set of footprints here, Sean, but not much else."

"Could be anybody's, boss. It's a public place."

Gardener sighed. "I know. Still, we'll have the tent up on this side first and photograph whatever we can."

Gardener rose and walked back around the outside of the building to go and speak to the team.

# Chapter Six

Gardener's team had assembled to the right of the building, the side with the gated entrance, allowing them all a bird's eye view of the scene. He'd love to have been a fly on the wall to the conversations.

The first thing he did was have a quick word with Fitz, the Home Office pathologist, to allow him to start almost immediately. He then turned and walked over to the team.

As he approached, they all greeted him in one form or another.

"Thanks for coming, guys. No need for me to explain what we found – you can all see for yourself."

"Is it suicide?" asked Colin Sharp, but the expression of disbelief on his face as he said it meant he already suspected the answer.

"Not from what we've seen," said Reilly.

"I realise that not every suicide leaves a note," said Gardener, "and it is possible Scenes of Crime might come across one. But we're still left with the question of how he got into that position by himself because from what little evidence we have, it isn't possible."

"No," said Frank Thornton, "it has to be murder, surely."

"Even so, that still leaves the question of how the hell *they* got him up there," offered Bob Anderson.

"Short of sneaking up on someone from behind," added Rawson, almost laughing, "on a set of stilts and throwing a loop over his head whilst lifting them off the ground, I'd say it's impossible."

"You could have a point," said Gardener.

"Looking at the place," said Anderson, "there's only two points of entry and exit. This gated end, or that end with the arched window. That might help us when we're looking for evidence."

"The other thought Sean and I had is that he may have been killed somewhere else and brought here."

"What makes you say that?" asked Thornton.

"The marks on the neck," said Gardener. "They appear to be different to a true hanging."

"That could make things awkward," said Rawson.

"He could be anyone from anywhere," said Sharp.

"Well, we know the answer to that one," said Gardener, relaying the conversation they had with Adi Giles. As he finished, he noticed DC Sarah Gates and PC Julie Longstaff roll up, park the car, and trot along to the scene.

"Oh my God," said Longstaff, "that's not a good start to the morning."

"For him, or you?" asked Anderson.

"Both," laughed Gates. "What the hell's happened?"

Gardener quickly summarised what he and Reilly had found before going on to explain the breakthrough in identifying the man.

"I can't imagine a publisher making too many enemies," said Longstaff.

"You'd be surprised," said Reilly.

"Going a bit far, isn't it," said Gates. "I didn't get my book published so I think I'll hang him."

"Make a great start to the killer's next book," said Rawson.

"Yes," laughed Longstaff, "that's proper research for you."

Keen to move things on, Gardener continued, "Anyway, guys, I'm afraid it's all the usual boring stuff for now."

He glanced around, studying the area. Although there *were* houses nearby, they were some distance away, across the A65 and either side of the visitor's centre. He turned back to the team.

"We'll have to plan out a house-to-house inquiry. Judging by where the houses are, I don't think anyone will have seen a great deal."

"No one ever does," said Anderson. "People living next door to each other never actually see anything half the time."

"That's true," said Gardener. "But the thing we have to consider for the moment is how many people were involved and how did they transport the body, especially if Knowles was killed somewhere else."

"My guess is a van," said Reilly, "probably a white one without a logo. After all, you wouldn't want to advertise what you were up to."

"We may strike lucky," said Gardener. "It's not beyond the bounds of possibility that someone saw something."

"Maybe two of us should nip down the road to that pub, The Vesper Gate," said Rawson, "see what was going on there last night?"

"Good idea, Dave," said Gardener. "See if any strangers were in drinking, or if anyone new has started using the pub more recently. You couldn't have carried this out without some form of planning."

"Maybe we should talk to the people who run the visitor's centre," said Gates.

"Yes," agreed Longstaff. "They must see a lot of people in a day. And they're just across the road. Maybe someone has been eyeing the place up more than usual."

"Another good idea, Sarah," said Gardener. "Maybe you and Julie can take that one."

As they nodded, Reilly made another suggestion. "We're gonna need to do all the usual inquiries with CCTV and that might be the best place to start."

Gardener studied the CCTV points. The abbey definitely had cameras but he wasn't sure where all of them were. If any of them actually covered the inside of the ruined church, that would be a real bonus.

"The other things to concentrate on once we have access are the body and the rope," said Gardener. "We need to check it for DNA. Hopefully someone will have left their prints on it."

"Wouldn't help us if they're not on file," said Anderson.

Gardener nodded. "I appreciate that, Bob, but it's worth a try – particularly on the body. Fibre taping and DNA on the cuffs and collar, there must be some evidence there. Chances are whoever did this, they know him."

"Do you want a couple of us over at the publishers?" asked Sharp.

"It's okay, Colin, we're planning to do that once we've finished here," said Gardener.

"Did the rope look new?" asked Gates.

"Not particularly," said Reilly. "Which does give us a problem trying to establish its origin."

"Knots will be something else to look into," said Gardener. "The noose looks pretty standard stuff, but it might be interesting to see what kind of a knot has been used around the beams in the ceiling. We can cut the rope from the beam but save the knot and take photos of it.

"I have Scenes of Crime and PolSa coming in for a fingertip search so hopefully they will be able to give us something to go on, but right now it's field work and old-fashioned policing – knocking on doors and asking questions."

Gardener glanced at his watch. Time was moving on. It was a Wednesday, which meant most people would be at work, so the chances of catching people early had probably been lost.

"Okay, it'll be a long hard day so the quicker we start the better."

As the team dispersed, chattering excitedly, he turned and faced the gate. Fitz was on the other side, about to come through.

"Did you find anything?"

The pathologist nodded. "The rope marks on the neck don't bear the inflamed edge of a vital reaction."

"Which means no struggle," said Reilly.

"It would seem that way," said Fitz. "Until I do a full autopsy there isn't much more I can tell you."

"Any idea on a cause of death?" Gardener asked.

"I think the man has been strangled somewhere else and then transported here for whatever reason."

"I realise it's not an exact science," said Gardener, "but any idea how long he's been dead?"

Fitz shook his head and took a deep breath. "Anything up to twelve hours. It's the best I can do for now."

"Better than nothing," said Reilly.

"Do you know who he is?" asked Fitz.

"We do," said Gardener, "and we know what he does for a living."

"Well that's a better start than you normally have," said Fitz. "Anyway, I'm happy for the body to be cut down and taken to the mortuary for a better examination."

Gardener nodded. Luckily for him, the SOCOs and the PolSa team were turning up and setting up.

Steve Fenton, the Crime Scene Manager, was heading his way. Fenton had short black hair, a rugged complexion and slim build. He was thirty-eight and married and lived pretty locally, in Farnley. His knowledge of the area would come in useful. Once Gardener had given him his instructions, he pulled his phone out of his jacket and called Patrick Edwards, the youngest member of the team. He asked if Patrick and Paul Benson could set up the incident room back at the station and call in the HOLMES team.

Finally, Gardener turned to his partner. "Right, let's go and see if we can catch up with the publisher."

# Chapter Seven

Gardener and Reilly were on Kirkgate. Adi Giles had been right, Kirkgate Chambers was to the left of the City Market's entrance, which was in a far better condition than the building on the right.

The exterior – finished in an old, faded grey emulsion that resembled the clouds above it – had seen better days. Gardener peered at the sign above the building's front door and could make out the words City Chambers.

There were four brass plaques on the wall at the side of the door. Three of them were highly polished: one belonged to a solicitor, another to an accountant, and the third to an interior designer. The fourth had a dull, tarnished finish, which belonged to Kirkstall House Publishing.

"Interesting place," said Reilly.

"That's just what I was thinking," replied Gardener.

He pushed open the front door. Inside, they were greeted by a long, winding staircase, with an odour of lavender and beeswax. A light green carpet covered the floor. Adorning the walls were a number of oils featuring Leeds city centre. The building had an office on each floor. Kirkstall House Publishing was at the top. The whole place was as silent as the grave.

Gardener grabbed the banister. "Let's go and see what we're dealing with."

As they reached the top floor, Gardener noticed the publisher's door was ajar. He opened it and slipped inside, with Reilly behind him.

The room had one desk with a swivel chair, a computer and a monitor, a number of filing cabinets and three more chairs. An old coffee table sat near two of the chairs, with a number of magazines and a large book covering the surface. The cord carpet was brown but appeared well kept despite its age. Tea-making facilities stood on one of the filing cabinets and someone had obviously done their best to make it feel homely because it smelled quite fresh. In the corner, Gardener noticed a door leading into another office.

"How the bloody hell should I know where he is, I'm not his keeper."

The voice had come from the other room. The sound was deep and gravelly, possibly a smoker's voice.

"I know you had a meeting with him yesterday afternoon. I'm not bloody stupid. I do run the place as well."

"Sounds like Cyril's in full flow," said Reilly.

"Unless it's Vera," offered Gardener.

"If it is," said Reilly, "I don't want to meet Cyril."

"Do you think he's on the phone?" asked Gardener. "Or dressing someone down in person?"

"We wait here long enough, we might find out. If he carries on talking like that they're liable to deck him."

Gardener nodded and waited.

"You could try ringing him yourself instead of giving me all this grief," shouted the voice.

A cracking sound then suggested that the phone had been slammed down.

"You should be careful how you speak to people," said a female voice.

Gardener glanced at Reilly. "Must be Vera."

"Are you still here? I thought I told you to go and get me something to eat."

"What did your last slave die of?"

"Answering me back."

Something crashed down in the office and the male voice suddenly shouted out, "Where the fuck is he?"

"You won't find out getting yourself all worked up."

"I'm not gonna find out at all, you are. Get him on the phone and ask him where the hell he is."

"It isn't my bloody job to find him," shouted the female, obviously storming toward the door, judging by the footsteps coming their way.

"And while you're at it, will you get me something to eat from Greggs."

The footsteps stopped but started again.

"And get me a newspaper."

Gardener saw the handle turn and the door move before the voice hit again. "And for Christ's sake get me something for this splitting fucking headache."

As she came through the door she quietly whispered, "How about an axe?"

She suddenly stopped dead at the sight of two possible clients.

"Oh, I'm so sorry. Can I help you?"

Vera was chubby, with strawberry blonde hair, desperately trying to hang onto any youth she had. Gardener figured she probably spent a lot of time at the hairdresser and manicurist. She wore an old-fashioned, beige two-piece suit of some quality, which spoke of M&S, as did her shoes.

"Are you Vera Purdy?" he asked.

"Yes."

"We'd like to speak to Cyril Knowles."

"Oh, I'm afraid he's far too busy to see anyone without an appointment, and I do all of those, so I know he doesn't have any spare time today."

Gardener and Reilly flashed warrant cards and introduced themselves.

Vera changed instantly and pointed to the door, as if she'd thought it would be a good idea to let them go through unannounced.

"Good luck with that one. He's in there, but watch how you go, he's a little sensitive this morning."

"We know," said Reilly, "we've heard."

Vera made for the outer door. "I'll be back in a few minutes. I have a list of things to fetch for his lordship, which you've no doubt also heard."

She left and they headed for the door into Cyril's office. The room was large, accommodating two desks and an inordinate number of files, which were conveniently stored on shelves, with the overspill left on desks and chairs. The place resembled the scene of a burglary. In the corner, on a cabinet, he also had tea and coffee facilities. The enclosed space smelled musty. Coupled with the grime on the windows, it would suggest they had never been opened.

"Who are you and what the hell do you want? I told her I didn't want to see anyone."

Cyril Knowles was small and wizened and appeared to be in his seventies, but Gardener doubted he was that old. He had very little hair and what he had was white, and brighter than his teeth; Gardener could smell his bad breath across the room. He was as thin as Max but unlike his brother, he was sporting rather bright, garish colours, in the shape of a green jacket, with a yellow shirt and green tie. Gardener couldn't see the trousers but he didn't want to.

Both detectives introduced themselves.

"I think you've got the wrong office. The solicitor is downstairs." Cyril stared back down at his paperwork.

"No," said Gardener, "it's you we want to see."

"Look, if it's about the parking ticket, I told one of your lot last week, I haven't had one. I can't pay for what I haven't had. I never parked there anyway."

"We don't do parking tickets," said Reilly.

Cyril sighed. "Well, if it's the speeding fine, the cheque's in the post."

"We don't do speeding fines either," said Reilly. "Proper little law breaker by the sound of things, aren't we, Cyril?"

"Maybe it's time you went then because I'm busy, seeing as I'm the only fucker in the office."

Instead of leaving, they both took a seat.

"This is harassment, if you weren't the coppers I'd call them."

"No one's harassing you, Mr Knowles," said Gardener, "we're trying to talk to you about something important."

"Well if you don't do parking and you don't do speeding, what kind of coppers are you?"

"I think you must have a hearing problem, we quite clearly said Major Incident Team."

"And there's been a major incident involving your brother," added Reilly.

"Well good luck with finding him this morning, no fucker else can. Last we heard he was leaving town with Lord Lucan and Shergar. Likes a flutter does our Max. He'll be shacked up with some tart half his age."

If Max was anything like his brother, Gardener doubted that, unless it was of the paying variety.

"Does he lose much?" asked Reilly.

"Show me someone who wins much and I'll show you a liar. Mug's game."

"Couldn't agree more, Mr Knowles," said Gardener.

"Anyway," said Cyril, finally staring at the two of them and putting aside whatever paperwork he had been studying. "What does major incident mean?"

"Mr Knowles, I'm really sorry to have to tell you but the major incident to which we're referring is the death of your brother."

The statement hit Cyril like a brick wall, because he didn't say anything at all. He didn't even blink. He merely continued to stare at them as if he hadn't heard them, or he didn't believe them.

Gardener was about to repeat what he'd said.

"Dead, you say?" asked Cyril.

The phone suddenly rang but Cyril ignored it. Instead he repeated the question.

"I'm afraid so."

"No, he can't be," laughed Cyril. "He was in here yesterday."

"Please rest assured, the man we found is your brother. We would like to talk to you about his movements, Mr Knowles."

After a short period of thinking, Cyril asked, "What happened?"

Gardener took him through everything.

The phone rang again.

"Vera," shouted Cyril, "answer the fucking phone, will you? Can't you see I'm busy?"

"Memory not what it used to be, Cyril, old son?" Reilly asked.

"What's that supposed to mean?"

"Only that you sent her out for something for that 'splitting fucking headache', as you called it."

"Oh shit!" Cyril rested his head in his hands.

"I realise it's a bad time, Mr Knowles, but we would like to ask some questions, if we can?"

Cyril nodded.

"You said your brother was in the office yesterday. Was he here all day?"

"He was here when I went, around two o'clock."

"How did he seem?"

"Same as usual. Plenty to do, spoke to lots of people about upcoming books, and one or two about new books." Cyril suddenly changed subjects. "You said you found him at the end of a rope?"

"That isn't quite how we put it," said Gardener, "but yes, he had been hanged. And I have to say we're very doubtful about it being suicide."

"Our Max wouldn't kill himself. He hasn't got the bottle."

"He's not been depressed about anything recently?"

"Max? No."

"So he hasn't attempted anything like this before?" Reilly asked.

"Like I said, he hasn't got the bottle, and he isn't depressed about anything."

"Has there been any trauma in his life recently: like a divorce, any problems?"

Cyril raised his hands and rubbed his bald head. "No, no, no. Like I said. Nothing's been bothering him and even if it had, he would never have done this. And he's not married."

"How is the business? Any problems, any threats, any dissatisfied customers?"

Cyril suddenly turned a little venomous. "All of them. You ever run a publishing house before? Everyone thinks they can write; everyone has a story to tell. Most of them have, and most are fucking garbage. Half of them couldn't even write a shopping list, let alone their life story."

"Are any of your customers dissatisfied enough to kill, then?" asked Reilly.

"We're a publisher, not the bleeding mafia. Who in his right mind would kill a publisher?"

Gardener let Cyril's rant pass. Although Cyril's temper was probably sharp most of the time, he *had* lost his brother.

The SIO then asked, "Can I ask where you were yesterday?"

"Oh, you think it was me now, do you?"

"Not at all, we're just asking where you were."

"I have an alibi, officer. I left early yesterday afternoon to meet up with an ex-Leeds United football player who was interested in writing his autobiography. We met at a restaurant in Leeds, had a meal and a few drinks, and I eventually got back home around ten o'clock."

"Where do you live, Mr Knowles?"

"Armley, within striking distance of the jail." Gardener wasn't sure if he'd added that last bit for fun. He asked for the correct address.

"And you didn't speak to Max at any time after you left yesterday?" asked Reilly.

"No," replied Cyril.

"Can you write down all the details for us, please, Mr Knowles," said Gardener. "The player you were with, the restaurant and your home address."

Cyril reluctantly did as Gardener asked, before Reilly added, "And the taxi firm."

"When would Max have left?" asked Gardener.

"I've no idea. It's our business so we work whatever hours suit. It's not a nine-to-five thing. Sometimes we're here quite late. But Vera would probably know."

As if on cue, they heard the outer office door close and Vera shouted she was back. Reilly stood up and slipped out of Cyril's office to speak to her while Gardener continued to question Cyril.

"Where does Max live?" Gardener asked.

Cyril supplied him with an address in Kirkstall. Before reaching for his phone, Gardener asked if he socialised in the area.

"Yes, loves the place. If you want Max out of office hours, you'll find him in The Vesper Gate."

Gardener noticed he was talking present tense. He tapped out a number on his phone and gave Dave Rawson all the details, which was handy because he and Colin Sharp were in the pub asking questions at that moment. When they'd finished in the pub, he asked them to call at Max's home address and see what they could find there.

"Does he have a mobile?"

"Oh, aye: mobile, laptop, tablet, or whatever you call them. I'm the stick in the mud, I hate the bloody things – all of 'em."

Without even having to be asked, Cyril wrote down his brother's number. Gardener then sent a text message to Dave Rawson with Max's number and asked him to try calling it when they were at the house.

"Does he drive?"

"No," replied Cyril, "he's a public transport man – mostly buses. Not taxis, they're too expensive. Other than that, he walks most places."

"Any close friends, or relationships?"

"No, a bit of a loner, is our Max. He mixes with plenty of people in the pub. Everybody in Kirkstall knows him but there's no one special in his life."

"You mentioned something about horses earlier, does he have a gambling problem?"

Cyril laughed. "He's too fucking tight to have a gambling problem. When he was sixteen, he won five pounds on the Pools, do you remember them?"

Gardener nodded. His father used to do them.

"He put that five pounds in a jar," continued Cyril, "and he started backing horses, using that money. If he won, he put it all in the jar, and only used the money from that jar. He won a few and he lost a few, but he still has that same jar at home. Only now it's got two or three hundred quid in it. He's watertight is our Max."

"Does he use a particular betting office?"

Cyril nodded. "Aye, Paddy Ashford in Kirkstall."

Gardener made a note. For now, he didn't think there was much else he could ask. Max didn't really sound like a rogue, but someone wanted him dead.

# Chapter Eight

Built in 1865, the Leeds City Varieties is a rare surviving example of a Victorian era music hall. The interior is a long rectangle, with plush red velvet seating, and cast-iron columns supporting two bow-fronted balconies. Famous names to have played the theatre include Charlie Chaplin, Marie Lloyd, and Houdini. Between 1953 and 1983, the theatre achieved national fame as the venue for the BBC television programme, *The Good Old Days*.

Tonight, the stage was playing host not to an escapologist, but the world-renowned hypnotist/illusionist, Mantra. Aged sixty, Mantra had been in the entertainment game all his adult life. He'd had a real passion for magic and illusions since the days of the TV personality, David Nixon. Shortly after leaving school he also studied hypnotism, and had been lucky enough to earn his living without ever having to do another job.

Standing to the left of the stage, he glanced out at the audience. It was a full house. People returned to the theatre time after time to see magicians and hypnotists, paid good money, and the only thing he could put it down to was the fact that they were desperate to see if they could figure out how the trick was done, or if it really *was* possible to hypnotise people.

"Thank you, ladies and gentlemen. Before we take a break for an interval tonight, I would like to welcome back to the stage my five guests."

During the round of applause, three men and two women walked on from the wings. Originally there had been eight but you couldn't put everyone under a spell. Some people simply refused to be hypnotised. As Mantra had not yet instructed them to do anything, no one took a seat.

He wondered about the younger of the two women, dressed in blue jeans and white blouse. She was still extremely nervous of being around Mantra. He sensed that it was not because she was on stage in front of a few hundred people, but more the fact that he was dressed head to toe in black: shirt, trousers, jacket and shoes, with a long cape that almost touched the floor; black on the outside, red on the inside.

By far the most frightening aspect for her was the tight black face mask. White lines outlined the shape of the face, and also crossed left to right, and it had holes for the eyes, nose and mouth. He'd sensed it the second she came onto the stage earlier in the evening. Masks could do that to people. Then again, it could be the voice. It was very unusual and despite being low and soothing, had a very raspy edge to it. He turned to the audience.

"I'm often asked, what is hypnotism? It's not an easy thing to explain to anyone, and let's be honest, why would I? If you knew what I know, I would be out of a job because nearly everyone in Leeds would be standing on street corners trying to hypnotise everyone they saw."

The audience laughed, so too did the contestants.

"Put simply," he continued, "at its core, hypnotism is all about the power of suggestion. It has two sides to it: a recipient being in a certain 'state' which can be termed 'a hypnotic state' but is basically a state where peripheral awareness is reduced and responsiveness to suggestion is enhanced. The other side is a hypnotist assisting the recipient to enter a hypnotic state and making suggestions for the recipient to act upon. The act of the recipient following suggestions made by the hypnotist is hypnotism."

Mantra moved to his left.

"Now we're all clear on that, I'll begin."

Another roar of laughter ensued.

He turned to meet the five people who were taking part in the experiment. Approaching the youngest male dressed in a tracksuit and trainers, he held out his right hand.

Milton Erickson, the father of hypnotherapy was famous for using the handshake technique as a way to induce the hypnotic trance. Two people shaking hands is the most common form of greeting in society. Used by a hypnotist, he shocks the subconscious by disrupting the common norm. Instead of shaking the hand normally, he would interrupt the pattern by grabbing the wrist, or pulling the subject forward and off balance, asking their names at the same time. With the pattern interrupted, the subconscious mind was suddenly wide open to suggestion.

You could have heard a pin drop in the theatre. He picked up on the fact that the audience was in fact more anxious than the contestants. They were dying to know what he was going to make them do.

"In a minute I am going to instruct each one of them individually, and when I snap my fingers for the first time, that person will fall under my spell. Then, I will speak to them again, as individuals, but I will do so by whispering in the ear. Therefore, you, the audience, will not actually hear what I am going to tell them to do. Are we clear?"

He was still facing the audience. Most of them agreed with him by simply nodding their heads, showing Mantra that he quite possibly had most of them under his spell as well.

He turned and approached the young man in the tracksuit and trainers. He held out his hand, the recipient took it and the hypnotist did exactly as he'd planned, pulled the man forward, told him to relax and asked his name, all while staring directly into his eyes and holding the position.

"Jason."

One down. Four to go.

He continued the pattern with each of them in turn, discovering a Lisa, and an Emily, she being the one who was most perturbed by the mask; but he certainly wasn't removing it. He then made contact with a Phil and a Henry, the latter being the oldest of the bunch at seventy-eight; fair play to him for being game.

Each of them sat. He turned to Emily. "Are you sad?"

"A little," she replied.

He drilled down a little further, asked one or two more direct questions, and then said. "Someone's left you, haven't they?"

The expression on her face was one of disbelief, as she frowned and her lips stretched wide in a grimace.

"Yes, my dog, Buster. How did you know?"

Mantra didn't answer the question but laid a hand on her shoulder and told her simply to relax and enjoy the experience and, if it helped, think about Buster and the pleasure he had brought her.

He faced the audience. "Are you all seated comfortably?"

No one said they weren't. "Then let us begin."

He faced the five contestants and spoke immediately to Jason. Staring into his eyes from about three feet away, he informed him that he was going to fall asleep very shortly, and that when he did and he heard the word 'hypnotism' his immediate reaction would be to tell the audience it was all fake.

Mantra clicked his fingers and caught Jason before he fell from the chair onto the floor, resting his head next to Lisa's shoulder. He followed the same procedure with all of them. Once he had everyone asleep he faced the audience.

"I was explaining to you about hypnotism," said Mantra.

"It's all fake," shouted Jason.

"No it isn't," said Lisa.

The audience suddenly started laughing. Mantra retreated to the side of the stage, watching the spectacle and the effect it was having on the crowd.

"It is," said Emily, pointing to Lisa. "She saw it all on YouTube."

"Who did?" asked Lisa.

"Aye, she knows all the secrets," said Henry.

"If it's secrets you want, you want to speak to her from Morris Grove in Kirkstall," added Phil.

"Who's she?" said Jason.

The audience was in complete uproar, pointing at the people on the stage, no doubt wondering how they could all have a conversation, as if it was the most natural thing in the world. Mantra smiled, as the conversation did not really make any sense to anyone, which was probably what made it so funny.

"She married one," said Jason.

"Aye, she disappeared in the bath one night," added Henry.

"She never saw herself again," said Phil.

"Neither did anyone else."

"Apart from the butcher on the High Street."

"Which butcher?"

"Which High Street? That's what I want to know."

The conversation between the contestants went on for a full ten minutes. It was complete gibberish, and topics of conversation went from hypnotists to soap operas, and finally finished up at UFOs.

Mantra snapped his fingers and shouted, "Wake up!"

The conversation stopped dead and all five contestants glanced at each other with expressions that basically said, "What the hell is going on here?"

The audience was beside themselves, laughing and pointing and rocking in their seats.

"Ladies and gentlemen," said Mantra to the contestants, "thank you so much for taking part tonight. I would like to assure all of you that there will be no lasting effects, and that you will not repeat any of what you have just said, or taken part in, again, no matter what phrases you hear."

The five contestants each bore a confused expression and were completely mystified as to what he was talking about. Mantra wished them all well and asked them to leave the stage and enjoy a nice cool beer during the intermission.

On the point of leaving the stage, Jason turned and shouted to the audience, "Anyway, I don't care what you say, it's all fake."

More screams of laughter erupted and even Mantra smiled. As they left the stage and mingled with the audience the house lights came up to signal the intermission.

Mantra stayed where he was, leaning against the right-hand side wall. One of the members of the audience, a man with no hair but a black beard, clasped and shook Jason's hand.

"Love it, son. Bloody great performance."

Jason smiled but had no idea why.

Blackbeard pointed his finger directly at Jason and shouted, "Hypnotism."

"It's all fake," shouted Jason.

"No it isn't," came another disembodied voice from another part of the auditorium.

Mantra noticed that was Emily.

Blackbeard suddenly stared at Mantra, as if to say, what's going on? Mantra smiled and shrugged his shoulders and headed for his dressing room, leaving Blackbeard, and perhaps some of the audience to wonder whether or not the spell really was still active.

# Chapter Nine

Gardener had gathered everyone together for an early start on the first incident room meeting connected to the murder of Max Knowles. He'd left them with quite a tall order of trying to gather as much information as possible in the shortest time.

Paul Benson and Patrick Edwards had done a great job in setting the room up with a number of tables and chairs and four whiteboards, the first of which was filling up nicely. HOLMES had set up in the next room; and he was feeling quite confident after he and Reilly had visited Cyril Knowles and listened to what he had to say.

"Thank you all for coming," said Gardener. "We have quite a lot to get through so I'll update you on the visit Sean and I made to the publishing house run by the Knowles brothers."

It took him around fifteen minutes to cover what they had discovered; all the while he was making notes on the whiteboard.

"Sean interviewed the secretary, Vera Purdy, while I was finishing off with Cyril Knowles," continued Gardener. "She said that Max was in good spirits yesterday: took a few phone calls, made a few, started to proofread a future publication, and finally left the office at four o'clock."

"She couldn't think of anyone who would want to kill Max," said Reilly. "Of the two, Max was the easier to get along with; he was calmer, easier to deal with. Cyril is a complete monster – her words. But she didn't think either of them were suited to dealing with people, or capable of running the business how it should be run. And each of them had a bit of a dark side."

"No wasted words there, then," said Colin Sharp, taking notes. "In what way were they dark?"

"She said that neither of them were beyond bending the rules a little, and they were often quite economical with the truth when it suited."

"All of which suggests the two of them may have upset someone enough to create an enemy," observed Frank Thornton.

"It would seem like it," said Gardener.

"Did Max tell Vera where he was going?" Bob Anderson asked Reilly.

"No, but he was pretty routine with his movements," answered Reilly, "so, the chances are he'll have done the same things as usual."

"Hopefully, this is where Dave and Colin come in."

Dave Rawson nodded and took the floor.

"Well, having just heard he left work at four, I'm not sure where he was for the next two hours but we know he turned up at The Vesper Gate shortly after six o'clock, where he *did* order his usual."

"Which was what?" Gardener asked.

"A big juicy T-bone steak with all the trimmings," said Colin Sharp, "and a bottle of red."

"A bottle?" repeated Gardener.

"Yes," said Rawson, "always a bottle."

"Did he drink it all?"

"He usually did," said Sharp, "according to the landlord. It generally took him all night, but he polished it off. He always finished his meal *and* had a dessert."

"Christ," said Reilly, "there was nothing on him. He can't have weighed eight stone wet through."

"Some people are lucky like that," said Gardener.

"So, just to recap what we know," continued Rawson, "Max Knowles left work at four, arrived in The Vesper Gate at six and stayed until ten."

"So we have the missing two hours to account for," said Gardener. "It's always possible it took him that long to reach The Vesper Gate, depending on which method he used."

"Was he by himself when he arrived at the pub?" Reilly asked.

"No, he was with friends," said Sharp. "We have their names, one was Tommy Parker, an old timer and a regular like Max. The other was Victor Smithson. We haven't spoken to them yet but they were with him most of the evening."

"Okay, see if you can catch those two today," said Gardener. "It's possible they can account for the missing two hours. How did Max seem?"

"He was fine, according to the landlord."

"Did he leave alone?"

"Yes," said Rawson, "but we know he never arrived home, so the last anyone saw of him was when he actually left the pub."

"Unless he passed someone on the way home," offered Reilly. "We should put out an appeal for witnesses."

"So where does he live?" asked Gardener.

"In a flat on Kepstorn Close."

"Where exactly is that?"

"About two miles away," said Sharp. "To get to his place, you leave the pub and turn left in the direction of the abbey. But then you leave the main road and take Abbey Walk."

Rawson took over. "But here's the thing. At the bottom of the walk there is a large open park with a children's playground. That divides Abbey Walk from Spen Lane, which leads to Kepstorn Close. He lives in the last block on the right. The flats are directly behind a row of houses that front Kirkstall Road, so it's very unlikely he was taken from there."

"It's more likely he was taken from that park you were on about," said Reilly.

"Is it all open around there?" Gardener asked.

"Some of it's open," said Rawson, "but there are areas with large clumps of trees, which would make it ideal to lift him."

"Don't suppose there was any CCTV?" asked Frank Thornton.

"Not that we saw," replied Sharp.

"Okay," said Gardener, "so that's the next area we need to canvas. Let's have someone round to these houses and ask the usual questions. According to Cyril, everyone in Kirkstall knew Max so you probably won't need photos but take them just in case.

"But I think the park is more important," Gardener continued, "so, let's shut down the entire park as a scene. We have enough reasonable grounds to suspect it contains evidence relevant to the investigation. I'll speak to DCI Briggs and hopefully bring in some operational support officers to help with this, and we'll have a full team in to do a fingertip search over the next few days."

Gardener wrote that on the whiteboard, and when satisfied, turned and asked another question.

"What about his flat, did you manage to have a look round?"

"Definitely," said Sharp. "The neighbour, Mary Bates, who lives in the flat opposite let us in. She was just leaving as we turned up."

"Leaving?" asked Reilly.

"It's not what you think," said Sharp.

"How do you know what I'm thinking?"

"Yeah, be fair," said Rawson to Sharp. "When does he ever think?"

"We definitely know *when* he's thinking," said Anderson, "we can smell the burning."

Even Reilly laughed, and then retorted, "You'll smell burning in a minute, sunshine; the speed I run across this floor and deal with you I'll leave scorch marks."

"Okay," said Gardener, smiling, "stop poking the bear, you'll only get hurt. What did you find out?"

"She has a spare key," continued Sharp. "She does a bit of cleaning for him. What is interesting is that she did not mirror Vera Purdy's words. Mary Bates spoke very highly of Max: he was always polite, always paid her on time. She often took him bits of baking and the odd bit of supper. She used to see him leaving for work in a morning. In the summer he would walk to the office, in the winter, he'd catch the bus."

"That should give us something to get our teeth into," said Gardener. "According to Vera Purdy he was a problem and could have brought on what happened to him. Mary Bates believed him to be a model citizen, but someone wanted him dead. Did she say anything else? Did anything about him ever concern her?"

"We didn't get that impression," said Rawson, "but until we start to dig deeper into his background, we won't know."

"So what was his flat like?"

"Clean, smelled fresh," said Sharp. "You could see his connection to the book world. There were hundreds of them, all around the flat. He seemed to have books on shelves in every room."

"Some were books he and his brother had published. Others were probably stuff he'd collected," said Rawson. "And he had a suitcase full of wrestling programs."

"Wrestling?" said Reilly.

"Yes, all that British stuff that was on TV years ago on a Saturday afternoon. He was definitely into sport because that's what most of the books were about: wrestling, boxing, football, rugby; all manner of sporting memorabilia."

"What about a phone?"

"Yes, we got that," said Rawson. "It was on one of his coffee tables, so he must have forgotten to take it with him."

"We dropped it into a Faraday bag and it's with the tech lads now."

"Excellent," said Gardener, "that might give us something to go on. We'll need to check the history, find out whom he spoke to. We also need to look into everything else: bank accounts, bills, landline telephone, digital footprints, anything that might give us a clue as to what was really going on in his life. Someone also needs to check out the bookie in Kirkstall, Paddy Ashford."

Gardener related the tale about the jar of money.

"We wondered what that was," said Sharp. "It looked out of place on one of the window ledges."

Gardener turned back to the whiteboards where he drew up a list of questions and quickly went through them.

"So, where was Max taken from? That's going to be the fly in the ointment because it could have been anywhere between The Vesper Gate and his home, but the most promising location would be the park. Next question, where was he killed?"

"Again," said Sarah Gates, "that could have been anywhere between the two destinations, but maybe the park is still the best option."

"Or," offered Julie Longstaff, "if the vehicle they transported him in was big enough, perhaps whoever had him, killed him in the vehicle."

"Good point, Julie," said Gardener. "We've already discussed the fact that it could have been a large van, so that would back up your point, but we're going to need coverage of CCTV and ANPR for that one, so that's a job for someone. Go through the ANPR and CCTV footage, see how many vans we can spot, compile the list, find out who owns them, and then start asking questions."

Gardener checked another question.

"What were his last movements? Well, until we get the answer to some of the above, we don't know that one for sure. That involves more house-to-house inquiries, but at least we have a distinct area to concentrate on. We know the houses that are clustered within two or three miles of the pub, and we know in which direction he was heading. Speak to everyone."

"It might be worth checking every house to see if it has a CCTV camera on the wall," said Gates. "We might just get something from that."

"Worth a go."

"Didn't you say something about his brother leaving the office early yesterday as well?" asked Paul Benson. "Where did *he* go?"

"I was just coming to that, Paul. He met up with an ex-Leeds United player. They had a meal at a restaurant and a meeting about a forthcoming autobiography." Gardener fished the details from a folder and passed them over. "That might be a job for you and Patrick. Contact the player and arrange to pay him a visit, do the same with the restaurant, and then pop along to Cyril's home address and speak to his neighbours."

"You want to know what he's like, sir?" asked Edwards.

"We know exactly what he's like, son," said Reilly. "We had a belly full of him yesterday." Reilly went on to tell them about the parking and the speeding fines that Cyril thought they were there to speak about, which generated quite a bit of laughter. "No, we want to see if his story checks out; most important, what time did he get home and did he stay there?"

Benson nodded. "Leave it with us."

A knock on the door paused the meeting.

# Chapter Ten

Desk sergeant Dave Williams dropped a folder in. "Autopsy results, sir."

Gardener thanked him. Williams left. The SIO scanned the document, which wasn't particularly thick.

"What do we have?" Reilly asked.

"Pretty much what we thought, Sean. Fitz believes he was killed by manual strangulation. There was evidence of petechiae – small red dots in the eyes – a definite sign. His best estimation of it happening was between ten thirty and eleven, which fits in with his possible movements. He hadn't soiled himself, another sign of him being killed prior to the hanging. There's plenty of technical stuff in there but that's what we really wanted to know."

"So why hang him?" asked Paul Benson.

"The only reason I can think of, Paul," said Gardener, "is to make an example."

"You don't think it's drug or gang related, do you?" asked Frank Thornton.

"Until we know more about his lifestyle I couldn't say," replied Gardener, "but I wouldn't have thought so. And even if he owed the bookie a lot of money – which looks very unlikely judging by the winnings jar – I doubt Paddy Ashford would go this far."

"Unless, for some reason, it's all for show," suggested Bob Anderson.

"Which brings us back to making an example of him," offered Longstaff.

"Maybe," said Gates, "or maybe this is someone who likes to put on a show, make a spectacle of others."

"Whoever it is," said Longstaff, "they're very confident. If they took Max in an open area and then hanged him in a public place."

"It all sounds very plausible," said Gardener, "so, when we delve deeper into Max's background we may find he's upset someone in the publishing world."

"What kind of stuff do they publish?" asked Anderson. "Didn't you say autobiographies of sport personalities?"

"That's what Cyril said – mainly people involved in sport."

"But they do digress now and again," said Reilly to Gardener. "When I spoke to Vera Purdy in the other office, you might remember seeing a coffee table with magazines and a book."

"I do," said Gardener.

"Well, I had a look at the book, it was one of those big coffee table productions. What made me pick it up was the photo of Kirkstall Abbey on the front. Anyway it's full of photos of strange, eerie places, and underneath each photo is a bit of history. I happened to notice on the back that it was one of theirs, Kirkstall House Publishing."

"That's interesting," said Gardener. "Cyril never mentioned that stuff, did he?" He turned to Gates and Longstaff. "Can you girls dig into the website and check their digital footprints, see what these guys were really into?"

"Love to," said Gates.

"Meanwhile," said Longstaff, "we have something interesting from the abbey CCTV."

"Sounds promising," said Gardener.

"Well, we had a look at two lots. Firstly the stuff from the visitor's centre. They have a number of cameras positioned all over the abbey, none of them pointing exactly where we wanted it, but there was one pointing toward the gated entrance."

"Was?" questioned Reilly. "Why do I get the feeling this won't finish up in our favour?"

Gates nodded. "We spoke to Vivienne Turner in the offices, because we didn't think the camera was angled properly when we saw it. It only showed the area leading toward the gate, and not the gate itself."

Longstaff took over. "She seemed to think it had been moved because it should be pointing *at* the gate, which once again leads us to believe that this is someone who knew the area, who knew what they were doing, and were very confident. They probably moved it to make sure they couldn't be caught out."

"What *did* it show?" asked Rawson.

Gates laughed and said to Rawson, "You're going to love this, it's right up your street."

A large projector screen had been set up on one wall, with a laptop plugged into it. Gates started the footage from the previous night. Two women were walking a dog when suddenly a man in a raincoat and a mask ran out and exposed himself. That brought comments, but what left the team in uproar was when the women were not fazed in the slightest and actually started throwing rocks at the flasher, who took off and smashed his knee into a wall.

The laughing then stopped when a flash of light lit up the interior of the ruined church, almost as if it was lightning. But they all knew that the weather on the previous night was calm and clear.

"What the hell was that?" asked Anderson.

"We don't know," said Gates. "We've studied it, and the only thing we can come up with is a flashbulb from a phone or a camera."

"What?" said Rawson. "As bright as that?"

"It *was* powerful," said Longstaff. "We're thinking a proper camera set-up rather than a phone."

It happened three or four times in succession and then stopped.

"How interesting," said Reilly. "So whoever our suspect is, they must have hung him and then taken photographs."

"A contract killing?" said Anderson. "Someone wanted him dead and they wanted proof?"

"That could well take us in a different direction," said Gardener. "Hopefully, the victim's background will give us a further clue."

"It's not the kind of thing a local publisher would get mixed up in, is it?" said Reilly. "Contract killings, gangs, drugs. I mean, this guy was just a local publisher who puts out sporting books by people who have been out of the game for some time and perhaps looking for a bit of extra money."

"I agree with you, Sean," said Gardener, "but maybe this has something to do with his dark side; so we need to find out how dark." Gardener turned to Sharp. "Did he have a computer, or a laptop, or a landline at home?"

"Yes," said Sharp. "Tech boys again, they're going through it, and we've spoken to BT about his landline."

Gardener nodded, and then thought of something else.

"Julie, Sarah, can you get back on to the abbey and see if any of their cameras point out onto the main A65 road? It's possible we'll see Max walking home." As he said it, he wrote it on the whiteboard.

He turned back to the team. "We will also need to try and look into the idiot who was exposing himself. He may or may not have anything at all to do with it, but he might have seen something."

"Hardly going to want to come forward, is he?" said Thornton.

More laughter circled the room.

"Who does that now?" said Rawson. "I thought with the introduction of the internet, you could get your rocks off in private without going to all that trouble."

"Is there something you're not telling us here, son," said Reilly.

Rawson laughed, taking the comment in good fun.

"It is a sensitive issue, though," said Benson. "Bob's right, this guy might have seen something but there's no way he's going to come forward, is he?"

Patrick Edwards was still giggling. "Can you imagine him coming to see us and then having to explain what he was doing at the abbey at that time of night?"

More laughter erupted, but was soon levelled when Rawson asked, "What's with the mask?"

"Oh, come on, son," said Reilly, "look what he's doing. He's hardly likely to show his face."

"I didn't mean that," said Rawson. "I was talking more about the mask itself. I've seen something like that before."

"Can we zoom in a bit?" Gardener asked Gates.

She did as he asked. They lost quality but it was enough to make out the design.

Rawson continued, "It's quite tight, hugs the face well. But look how distinctive it is with the oval white lines outlining the face, and then crossing left to right across it: with holes for the eyes, nose and mouth. I reckon that's pretty specific."

"You're right, Dave," said Gardener.

He added it to the whiteboard and then turned. "Can we get a printout of that for the board? Let's have someone looking into local flashers; they obviously still exist. And see if we can chase down the mask. It is specialist stuff – where is it sold, who's bought it, that kind of thing. The likelihood is, only one of those masks belongs to our man in this area so it's possible *we* might find *him*, rather than hoping he comes to us."

"There is something else we can do," said Reilly.

"Go on," said Gardener.

"We've put out appeals in the past for witnesses who we know shouldn't be doing what they were doing at the time. Do you remember the armed robbery at a supermarket in Pudsey?"

"Oh, yes." Gardener nodded. "The CCTV showed someone in the background shoplifting, but they looked like they got a good look at one of the robbers."

Reilly continued. "What we did was put out a press release saying we were investigating a very serious offence and we were looking for a particular witness who, at the time, may have been committing a lesser offence for which we were not looking to prosecute."

"Indecent exposure is a bit different from shoplifting," said Gardener. "We could still do it but we'd have to follow protocol. We need to try to find the victims – the people flashed at, and get their permission to not charge the offence. Equally we'd have to get the CPS to agree that it's 'not in the public interest to prosecute'.

"Doing it this way, we might get the witnesses to come forward, particularly if we use a third-party intermediary so his identity remains unknown to the police."

"Problem is," said Reilly, "any information obtained this way will be intelligence and not evidence."

"True," said Gardener, "but it might point us in the right direction."

Gardener then addressed Gates and Longstaff again. "You said you had two lots of CCTV, what's the other?"

"Maybe something and nothing," said Longstaff, "but that picture you have up there, is it Adi Giles, the man who found Max Knowles?"

"Yes," said Gardener, "why, you haven't found him somewhere at the abbey that raises suspicions, have you?"

"No," said Gates, "but we did run the CCTV on Kirkgate, which actually gives us a pretty good view of the publisher's office. Adi Giles walked by."

"When?"

"On the day in question, sometime in the afternoon," said Gates. She grabbed a folder and retrieved a document. "Here it is, about lunchtime, just after twelve thirty."

"Did he go into the publisher's office?" asked Gardener.

"No, just walked by," said Longstaff. "We're not suggesting anything, just that it seemed ironic that he should be involved in the investigation and then we see him on CCTV in an area that's still connected to the investigation."

"Fair point," said Gardener. "Doesn't prove anything, but it would be worth asking the question of where he was going."

"Did it show Cyril leave at two, and Max at four?" asked Sharp.

"Yes," said Longstaff. "We didn't specifically set out to look for it, but Sarah noticed there were cameras on Kirkgate so we thought it was worth checking."

"Well done," said Gardener. "Which direction did they leave in?"

"Cyril came out of the building and got straight into a taxi," said Gates. "Max left later but he turned and walked in the direction of Wellington Street, so he was probably heading for the bus station."

"Even so," said Gardener, "see if we can pick him up anywhere else."

Gardener was about to wind things up when another knock on the door interrupted them. Steve Fenton walked in with a file and a couple of clear evidence bags.

"Just in time, Steve. I take it these are from the scene?"

"Yes. Some interesting stuff here. Definitely thought you might like to see it."

He held up the first bag containing the rope.

"Nothing much here. Standard rope, it doesn't look new. It was tied to the beam using a reef knot, which is pretty common. Photos for the board of everything you need are in here." He placed the folder and the bags on the table.

"Any prints from it?" asked Reilly.

Fenton nodded. "Yes, but I'll come back to that. We decided to use a digital pressure scanner at the scene and it managed to lift prints from a pair of trainers. Photos of the tread are in the file so you might be able to work with it."

"Only one set of footprints?" asked Gardener.

"That's all we found."

"Surely it's not possible," said Reilly. "That suggests only one person was present at the scene. He couldn't possibly have hanged the man by himself."

"He *was* dead before he was hanged," suggested Anderson.

"Even so," said Gardener, "Sean has a point. Whilst it might be possible to do it alone, it is a lot of work for one man. Would be much easier with two."

"Even if one was only a lookout," suggested Reilly.

"And we also have to consider how he got Max to the scene," said Gardener. "Wouldn't have been easy on his own. Surely someone would have spotted something odd."

Steve Fenton added his bit. "Put like that it does sound a tall order, so maybe there *were* two. Perhaps one of them was clever enough to be suited and booted, or maybe he just had shoe coverings."

"Makes sense," said Gardener. "But that suggests the other person may have been in control. How could one suit up and the other not notice and question it?"

That brought a stilted silence to the room. It was a good point worth keeping in mind.

"However," said Fenton, holding one of the evidence bags aloft. "There is a hair in here. Maybe something, maybe nothing, when you consider how many hundreds of people visit the abbey in a day. The hair may not belong to our suspect but it's worth seeing if we can DNA it and trace it."

Gardener realised it was a needle in a haystack but it had to be considered. Even the smallest piece of evidence had been used to convict killers.

"Okay, Steve, well done. As Tesco keep saying, every little helps. But now I want to come back to what you're not telling me."

"The fingerprints," said Fenton.

Gardener nodded.

"You won't like it."

"On the contrary, son, that's why we do this job," said Reilly. "We love it."

"We love every aspect apart from this one," said Gardener. "I can tell by the look on his face we won't like this."

Fenton nodded. "We have prints from the rope and the scene. We also found prints on the cuff and collar of Max's suit."

"Are those prints in the system?"

"Surprisingly, yes," said Fenton.

"Let's have it," said Gardener. "Who do they belong to?"

"One Charles Lutwidge Dodgson, otherwise known as Lewis Carroll."

"Lewis Carroll, the author? Hardly a killer, was he?"

"No, but he was once suspected of being Jack The Ripper."

"Give over," said Reilly.

"I don't think anyone took it seriously, he was only suspected based on anagrams."

# Chapter Eleven

Adi Giles was sitting in a house on Hangingstone Lane in Ilkley that he couldn't possibly afford even in his wildest dreams. Though he hadn't actually seen them, he'd been assured it had five bedrooms, and most of those were en suite. The ground level had two reception rooms, a sitting room and a dining room, and there was even a wine cellar under the floor, and supremely coloured gardens as far as the eye could see. It was palatial by anyone's standards.

He was scared stiff to actually touch anything. The carpets were thicker than anything he had stepped on, and there were paintings hung on the walls that were probably worth more than his entire house. In some respects it was a cluttered room as there were ornaments and jugs and silverware all over the place but it was incredibly clean. He wouldn't have liked the responsibility of that job.

Something classical piped its way around the room as Mantra wheeled a tray through from the kitchen, which contained everything one needed for afternoon tea and biscuits. If he thought Adi was going to touch those, he was mistaken. They would probably disintegrate before they touched his lips and you'd be finding the crumbs for weeks. No, he wasn't going anywhere near them. Quite how he was going to manage the drink he wasn't sure.

"Please relax," said Mantra.

Easy for him to say, thought Adi, who was here for some private therapy from Mantra to help to try and control his anxiety, something Adi had had to live with since his school years. In fact, as far as he was concerned – and it had been hinted at during the first session they'd had – an incident at school was probably at the root of his feelings.

He'd known from an early age that he was different to other children, and that his sexual feelings towards other pupils were never directed toward females. He had been caught in a compromising situation in a stationery cupboard, not with a teacher, but another pupil of the same sex. From that point on, life had been unbearable for the pair of them. He'd been constantly teased about it and on many occasions chased and beaten up before making it home.

He'd never been able to deal with it then, and he struggled now. But his problems were not about being gay.

We were living in different times and most people he met were very understanding and didn't really care about it. They respected him for the person he was and what he could bring to their lives.

No, his worries now were everyday things: would he earn enough money to pay the bills, was Freddie okay, given where he worked, was his van in good running order? Would it start when he jumped in? Would it break down? Would he have enough money to buy food, was he eating the right food? Being a vegan helped, or so he thought.

Every bloody thing in life was a worry. There simply wasn't anything he didn't worry about. Which is why he needed expert help.

Mantra sat down, poured the tea and put a cup on the coffee table next to him.

"Did you find our last session of any help?"

Adi glanced at the man. He cut quite a cloth. Though his clothes were reasonably old, and black throughout, they were of excellent quality. Adi knew that Mantra wore a mask during his performances on stage but couldn't for the life of him think why he would wear it at home. *Did he wear it all the time? Was it uncomfortable? Did he have to wear it because of something medical?* Christ, thought Adi, I'm worrying about shit that doesn't even concern me now.

He realised Mantra was still actually waiting for answer to his question. "Oh, I'm so sorry."

"Take your time," waved Mantra, sipping his tea.

That was when Adi suddenly noticed that he actually wore black gloves. They were thin, like a surgeon's, but made from cotton.

"I'm so sorry," said Adi, apologising again, "you asked me a question. I was okay, after the session."

"Good. How did it help?"

"Well, strangely enough I did stop worrying about things for a short while." And he had. He was not lying. His mind felt a lot calmer for a day or two.

"So, hypnotising you helped," said Mantra, "in fact, it helped both of us, because I managed to find out the reasons for your problem, why you suffer from anxiety, but we now need to continue with that therapy and see if we can stop you worrying about everything under the sun."

"How the hell do we do that?"

"Have faith," smiled Mantra, "finish your tea, and then we'll start."

Adi Giles stared at the cup, wondering how he would complete the task of raising it to his lips without spilling it all over the place.

In order to divert his thoughts he found himself wondering about Mantra's physical features. He could see his lips, and when they parted, the teeth were clinically white. The man's nose was quite large and slightly crooked. His eyes were very dark, almost black, possibly the one feature that would be enough to unbalance you. *Did he wear the mask because he was ugly?* If he did it would have to be pretty bad. The ugliest person he'd seen was John Merrick, the Elephant Man, and he never wore a mask, so Mantra couldn't be that bad, surely.

"I can tell that you are on edge," said Mantra. "You seem very upset about something in particular, rather than everything. Has something happened recently?"

Adi suddenly relived the moment in Kirkstall Abbey. When he came across the hanging corpse of Max Knowles it was all he could do to stop his bowels completely erupting. His stomach lurched; he found it difficult to breath. His vision even started to blur. His emotions caved in and a zillion questions flew into his mind.

"Please tell me."

So Adi did.

"Dear me," said Mantra, "that must have been terrifying. And you knew the man. How awful for you? When did you find him?"

"A couple of days ago. I was going for a photo shoot. I know I like to photograph strange, eerie places, but I didn't expect to find something like that."

"And you've kept it bottled up since?"

"Yes," said Adi Giles, "I didn't know what to do. I've been out of my mind: I can't think properly, can't sleep; can't eat. I'm worried about Freddie and where he works. I'm also worried about the police. I've never been in trouble with the police before."

"Well you're not in trouble now," replied Mantra. "You found a dead man and you did the right thing because you called them immediately. You left the scene, you didn't touch anything, and you waited and answered their questions."

"I didn't have the bloody strength to leave."

"Nevertheless, you're not in trouble, Mr Giles."

Adi Giles reached out for the cup to drink his tea but then thought better of it.

"Is there something wrong with your tea?"

"No."

"Then go ahead, drink it."

Adi hesitated. "Look, I know this is stupid, but what if I drop the cup? Your carpet probably cost more than my house."

"It's only a carpet. Besides which, it has been stain treated. You could drop a gallon of blood on it and within ten minutes you would not know it had been dropped."

"Oh my good God."

"I'm sorry, I didn't mean to startle you. I wanted to assure you that you had nothing to worry about. Please, go ahead, drink your tea."

After a sip he felt the need to open up about a small problem he'd had when he was twelve. He told Mantra all about a shoplifting incident.

Mantra smiled. "I wouldn't worry about that. That was at least twenty years ago. The shop has probably been demolished and I doubt the police are still looking for you."

"There was another incident. I was in a gay club in Leeds when I was eighteen and the place was raided for drugs."

"Were you arrested, or charged?"

"No, I slipped out of the back."

"Were you carrying anything; were you taking drugs?"

"God, no." Adi Giles covered his mouth with his hands. "No, I've never taken anything like that."

"Nothing to worry about, then."

"But what if someone had told on me?"

"If they had, you'd have been spoken to by now."

Mantra placed his tea on the trolley and stared into Adi Giles' eyes. "I can help you but I need you to completely relax."

"I'll try. Honest, I will."

"Good," said Mantra, "I'm sure you will. Drink your tea and then sit back in the chair. Listen to the music. I'm going to put you into a trance and help to deal with the things that are bothering you. Three key things happen when you're under hypnosis.

"There is a drop in activity in the dorsal anterior cingulate cortex, the part of the brain stimulated when you're worried about something. It is less active during hypnosis. There is an increase in connectivity between certain areas of the brain, specifically the dorsolateral prefrontal cortex or DLPFC. That part of the brain is responsible for planning and organisation. And the insula, the part designed to help regulate body functions.

"And there is a decrease in connectivity between certain areas of the brain, this time between the DLPFC and a part of the brain concerned with self-reflection."

"God," said Adi Giles, "that's a bit much for me."

"You must excuse me. I am too technical for my own good, sometimes. In plain English, under hypnosis, people are more relaxed and more worry-free. There is a stronger connection between the brain and the body. People are less inhibited and will do silly or embarrassing things without thinking about it. These changes help to demonstrate how it is possible for people under the influence to feel less stress, less pain and less anxiety while under hypnosis."

"Is that why we see people dancing around a stage like a chicken?"

Mantra laughed, a very strange sound indeed, as if he desperately needed to clear his throat.

"You have it in one. By removing our inhibitions, we can achieve amazing things."

Adi placed his cup on the coffee table. He was so pleased that he had managed such a simple act all by himself, without creating Armageddon.

"Are you ready to try?"

Adi nodded.

# Chapter Twelve

On the large TV screen in front of him, Ronnie was controlling the character of a computer game called Hungry Horace; a fat, round little bubble on legs – a bit like Ronnie.

The action intensified when he spotted the guard. Ronnie started to sweat, bending the joystick all over the place, and actually moving in and out of his seat as if that would help.

It was a stupid fucking game, thought Ronnie. There were four levels and Horace's job was to enter the maze and gather food from around the park before leaving for the next section, whilst avoiding the park guards.

They were bastards; they were faster than Horace. When you thought you were clear and ready to enter the next level, they would float in and leave a cherry. Problem with that was, Horace suddenly took over, and you simply had to risk life and limb to grab the cherry: more food, more points. It had to be done. But then they would almost always catch you. It *was* possible to collect a bell to panic the guards, render them vulnerable. A bit like the power pills in Pac-Man.

"Oh, Jesus," shouted Ronnie, swerving out of the way by the skin of his teeth.

He clearly remembered the day he found the aged Commodore 64, with hundreds of games, and a C2 tape loader. It was in a charity shop. Even they were throwing it out because it was so old; no one else wanted it. But it worked perfectly. The shop manager was loading it into the skip as he walked by. Ronnie offered to pay but the manager refused. Ronnie took him at his word and did not donate anything – not that he ever had any intention.

The alarm suddenly sounded as the park keeper caught up with the little bubble, and Horace was no more.

Game Over!

"You bastard!" shouted Ronnie, jumping out his chair and launching the joystick. He was almost on a record score.

He stared at the words, seething. Game over was pretty much about his level of understanding where the three Rs were concerned. He could never understand why they called it that. All three words started with a different letter, and they said *he* was dyslexic. And that was another fucking tongue trembler. Even people who could read and write couldn't spell that word. Did they do it on purpose?

As the years passed, Ronnie had managed to teach himself to read and write a little, if only to make sure he could draw his benefits. It wasn't the sort of thing you would admit in his day, or to anyone. You couldn't ask someone for help to read and write because it was embarrassing; so people in such a situation often ended up teaching themselves in a manner of speaking. Didn't help with computer games, though. You simply had to dive in head-first and pick the game up.

"Shit!" Ronnie sat back down, his attention drawn to the dog-eared business card on the table. Two days he'd had it; two days in which he had constantly considered his options. There probably weren't that many. Ronnie pinched the bridge of his nose, like he usually did when he was in a quandary. *When wasn't he in one?*

His right leg was jerking like a ticking time bomb. He quickly smoothed down what little hair he had and jumped off the battered seat and scurried to the window. Staring out at the massive pile of shit he called a garden did nothing to alleviate his mood so he turned and glanced at the card again.

What to do?

"Calm down, Ronnie. You'll never think it out if you don't calm down."

He strutted into the kitchen, another bomb site. Pots and pans littered the sink and the draining board. Quite why, he had no idea: he rarely cooked and if he did it was usually a ding meal that he'd managed to acquire, either from the supermarket shelf or, if security were flapping around, the skip behind the building.

Ronnie opened the fridge. He grabbed the bottle of beer – his last. It didn't have a twist top, which resulted in his mood bordering nuclear when he couldn't find the bottle opener. Time passed before he realised it was in the living room next to the empty bottle he'd finished earlier.

Top off, lager tingling his taste buds, Ronnie started to think, whilst studying the card once more.

Here's what he knew.

Firstly: there was the little incident at Kirkstall Abbey, the one when he decided to show two dykes his birthday suit. The police now knew about that because it was in the newspaper – and he knew about it because he'd lifted the paper from the high street in Bramley earlier in the day.

He nearly laughed his tits off when he saw the appeal, and the fact that the police would like to speak to the two women involved, and if they were in complete agreement of not naming names and no prosecution, they would like *him* to come forward and tell them what he saw that night. The only reason he knew that was not because he had read it, but because he'd seen the appeal on one of the local news programs.

Well they could fuck that off. No prosecution – who were they kidding? Did they think there was something wrong with his head? That he would willingly turn himself in so he could tell them what he saw? Well, there was something wrong with his head, but it couldn't be fixed. He'd known that for years. His mother dying at five hadn't helped. A year later, he and his sister were taken into care because of another incident involving his father, whom he hadn't seen since.

He'd tried his best to block that one out of his mind but every now and again he had a meltdown, and it all came pouring out. Like, he'd thought, his head wasn't fixable.

Secondly: what he saw, or thought he saw.

Now that was interesting. He stared at the card again.

According to the news, the two women had mentioned a flashing – of lights, not the obvious one – but they couldn't tell the police what the hell it was all about. They had no idea. Simply picked up the dog and shot out of the place faster than the fucking guards chasing Horace.

He remembered trying to leg it before he smashed his knee into a wall, causing horrendous pain, the type that makes you grit your teeth and stop breathing. But whatever was happening he had to ignore it, so he'd hobbled off around the building like the Hunchback of Notre Dame.

But given that Ronnie was quite inquisitive, he actually stuck around to see what the flashing lights were all about.

That was what had caused his two-day dilemma.

Someone had been hung. And someone else was taking photographs. Of the corpse! *What kind of a fucking ghoul does that?* Ronnie couldn't make out who was taking them because the man had a camera in front of his face. However, when the flashbulb lit up the whole scene, Ronnie was pretty sure he caught sight of someone else standing in the shadows. But he couldn't see who that was either. Great fucking private eye he'd make.

That's when he decided he really didn't want any part of what was going on in there and legged it. After making it back to his car he sat in the driver's seat and listened to some music. Half an hour passed, and he calmed down enough to perhaps saunter back into the abbey and check if anything was still going on.

It hadn't been. Everyone appeared to have cleared out by then – apart from the corpse. And he certainly wasn't going anywhere. *But where had they gone?* Ronnie hadn't seen anyone leave.

That's when he had found the card. It was on the ground outside the gate, the opposite side to where he had been spying on them. Of course, it may have nothing whatsoever to do with anything. But he doubted it.

Thirdly: the dilemma – what to do?

There was only one thing for it. He stared at the card, took another large gulp of beer and grabbed his mobile. It was time for a payday.

He dialled the number whilst swigging more of the beer, to loosen his tongue up a little.

It was answered after three rings.

# Chapter Thirteen

An air of expectation presided over the incident room, and Gardener was as excited as any of them. It had been a long day, they'd started early, and evening was now approaching. As the team filed in, most of them carried a cup of something; judging by the smell, soup was the popular choice: apart from Reilly, whatever he had was wrapped in pastry but he wasn't letting anyone close enough to see what it was all about.

"Okay, guys, thanks for coming," said Gardener. "Hopefully, we have a lot to get through so let's start at the park."

Dave Rawson took to the floor. "We haven't really found anything yet. It was all sealed off by mid-morning and the search team started pretty much straight away. As you can imagine, there's a lot of stuff on there that doesn't look connected in any way, but it all needs to be examined and you know how long that could take."

"I realise that," said Gardener. "I suppose I was hoping for a lucky break."

"Depends on how you look at it," said Colin Sharp. "We have spoken to quite a few people, and some remember seeing Max, either passing by the house, or in the case of one person, she actually spoke to him."

"Go on."

"Most of the sightings happened on Abbey Road," said Rawson. "The last person he physically spoke to was a Mrs Joan Harris; lives at a place called Applewick House, almost the last one on the road. She was outside having a fag when he passed around ten fifteen. He nodded and said hello. They spoke about the weather and the usual stuff for a minute or so and off he went."

"That being the time," continued Sharp, "it would have put him close to the Abbey Walk turn off. So from there, it's pretty desolate till he reaches the park."

"And no one else reported seeing or speaking to him after that point?"

"Not that we've spoken to," said Rawson. "So by the time he made it to the park, and possibly across it, we'd be looking at ten thirty."

"But we did get something from one of the people who lives on Spen Lane. It's quite a long road that stretches both sides of the park."

"Did they see him?" asked Reilly.

"No," said Rawson, "they didn't see *him* but they saw a van. Bloke's name is Martin Forrest. He was putting rubbish out around ten thirty and he saw the van. Problem is it was too dark and too far away to identify it but he did say it wasn't white."

"But he couldn't confirm the size," said Sharp. "He said it wasn't big but it wasn't small, either."

"Great," said Reilly, "that really narrows it down."

"Well at least it gives us something to go on with CCTV and ANPR," offered Gardener. "If we can rule out white vans, that might give us a bit of scope. So if someone can keep trawling the cameras and compiling the list, we might strike lucky."

Gardener clocked Patrick Edwards making notes; he would obviously follow that one up.

"What about his two friends from the pub?" asked Gardener. "Did they have anything to add?"

"Not a lot," said Sharp. "They both live quite close to the pub so they were easy enough to find. Tommy Parker said Max was in there most nights. Always had a meal and a bottle of wine, usually left about ten."

"His mates always stayed till closing time," added Rawson. "Now both of these guys were sportsmen but not in the professional leagues and certainly not enough to write a book about it all."

"What did they do?"

"Victor Smithson played football for Pudsey Town, and Tommy Parker – believe it or not – was a wrestler."

"That subject's cropping up quite a bit," said Bob Anderson.

"Yes," said Rawson, "but he wasn't a pro, although he did make it onto the TV once. Apparently it was filmed at the Rothwell Leisure Centre, and he fought a well-known comedian of the ring, Les Kellett. But that was it, really. Both confirmed they met up with Max around six and that he was talking ten to the dozen on the night. He had one or two contracts for books in the bag so everything was well."

Gardener sighed inwardly – nothing there. He added the notes to the whiteboard.

"I suppose we'd better talk about Cyril, and his alibi, though I suspect that is watertight."

"Definitely," said Paul Benson. "As we know, he caught a taxi outside the office in the afternoon and went into the centre of Leeds: the footballer, the taxi driver, the restaurant manager and a waiter all confirmed where he was and at what time. They met in the Queens Hotel bar and stayed there until around six o'clock. They ate in the restaurant, and the same taxi picked Cyril up around nine thirty and took him home."

"He got back around ten and according to the neighbours he was at home till the next morning, where – in their opinion – he no doubt topped a skinful of ale with even more before collapsing in a seat."

"That sounds like they've had problems with him before," said Gardener.

"One or two," said Benson, "but it was nothing serious. He liked a drink and when he'd had a few he got rowdy. He has the Dixons on one side and the Johnsons on another."

"Did they get on with him?"

"Not really," said Edwards, "Mr Dixon doesn't like him, and Mrs Dixon tolerates him. The Johnsons don't actually see a lot of him to comment. They work in finance in the city and the house they have is only a stopgap until some fancy new apartments are finished."

"Bet they're loving that," said Reilly, laughing. "A view of the prison beats a scenic city view any day, so it does."

"If you want a character reference," said Benson, "he was bigoted, racist, loud-mouthed and liked his own way."

"No surprise there, then," said Reilly.

"Thing is, boss," said Frank Thornton, "even though his alibi is rock solid it doesn't mean he didn't have anything to do with it."

"But why would he, Frank?" asked Gardener. "What does he stand to gain? A half share of a publishing outfit that are not breaking records anyway."

"Maybe not, but it would still be a half share he didn't have."

"It's a good point," said Gardener. "His alibi has to stand. I can't see three or four people all confirming it if there was something dodgy in it. I can imagine one person might lie but not all four."

"Has he hired someone?" asked Julie Longstaff.

"It's a possibility," said Reilly, "but I reckon Cyril's far too tight for that."

"Interesting though," said Gardener. "The only way we'll find out is by digging into the business itself. I know you were looking into it, but I'll come back to that later, I just want to try and touch on the other stuff we have listed. Does anyone have anything on the rope?"

On the subjects of the rope, the trainers and the hair, everything they had was in the negative. The rope yielded nothing. Forensics had found some prints but they once again belonged to Lewis Carroll, which was a point that really needled Gardener.

"How is that possible?" he asked.

"I'm following up on that, sir," said Rawson. "It seems you can get gloves off the internet with celebrity fingerprints. Elvis is very popular, drives the SOCOs mad."

"Who the hell came up with an idea like that?" asked Reilly.

"More to the point," offered Thornton, "who the bloody hell would buy them?"

"Criminals, obviously," said Anderson.

"Okay, Dave, keep on with that one. If you can find the name of the company, we may get a lead on who bought them."

Rawson nodded.

Further points noted that the footprints found at the scene were incredibly common. They belonged to a size eight trainer, most probably Adidas and most likely sold all over the world, so that was another needle in a haystack. The DNA sample of the blond hair had been fast-tracked but there was nothing on record.

"Did anything come from the appeal with the flasher?"

"Yes," said Gates. "The two women in the abbey on the night in question were Greta Swazlowski, and her partner, Anne Wilson."

"They were still howling with laughter about it this afternoon," said Longstaff. "They're happy for us to look into it, they're not pressing charges and they don't mind if we give them a mention. Said it was the best laugh they'd had in years."

So too, it seemed, in the incident room. When the laughter finally died, Gardener asked if the ladies had elaborated on what had been the origin of the flashing light within the ruined building.

"No," said Gates, "that was a step too far. It really spooked them. Not so much the light itself, but they weren't prepared to hang around and see what *was* going on."

"Why were they out so late, did they say?"

"Yes, they both work the nightshift for Asda in Pudsey. They're involved in goods inwards and don't start till two in the morning. Apparently they like to take the dog for a walk, and the abbey route is a favourite place. They like it, and it's pretty quiet."

"Do they live in Kirkstall?"

"No," said Longstaff. "Pudsey, they usually drive out and then back before starting work."

"Okay, the very least we can hope for is that the flasher will come forward," said Gardener, but he thought it was doubtful. He was still a little disappointed that nothing positive was forthcoming.

As he turned from the board, Rawson put his hand in the air. "Coming back to the flasher we might have some luck with the mask. Like I said, it is a bit specialised."

"Go on," said Gardener.

"I was talking to Bob and Frank earlier. They'd been to see Vera Purdy. When they got back they started leafing through the wrestling magazines that Max had."

"Oh, yes," said Gardener. "I'll come back to you two about Vera Purdy but for now we'll stick with the mask."

"One of our British wrestlers in the seventies, passing himself off as Japanese, used to wear them. I think there were four colours: red, black, purple, and I forget the other one but they were identical to the one the flasher wore."

"I think I remember him," said Reilly. "Never took it off, apparently."

"Okay," said Gardener. "Can you buy them online?"

"Not from what I can see," said Rawson. "You used to be able to at one time, probably when he was a big player on telly but not anymore."

"So our flasher might have had his for years," observed Gardener.

"More than likely," said Rawson.

"What about the wrestler himself?" asked Reilly. "Was there a link to him anywhere?"

"I didn't really check," replied Rawson, "but if he was around in the sixties and seventies, he's likely to be long gone now."

"Worth a try, Dave, you never know what we might learn."

"I'll look into it."

Gardener nodded but he was still searching for the piece of gold. "What did Vera Purdy have to say?" he asked Bob Anderson.

"Well, we were looking at the notes from yesterday and thought it was worth a follow up."

"Was Cyril in?" Reilly asked.

"He was," said Thornton, "but he didn't show his face. Just shouted his instructions through the wall."

"Sounds like him. So what did she have to say?"

"She's bloody frustrated," said Anderson.

"What do you mean?" asked Gardener.

"She really likes what she does, but she feels she can do a far better job than either of them put together."

"She keeps coming up with ideas for the business but they're not interested," said Thornton. "She reckons she would keep the autobiographies but she'd branch out with other stuff."

"So it's the brothers Grimm that frustrate her," said Reilly.

"Yes," said Anderson. "She's not keen on the way they handle things. They don't offer advances unless forced. They're not very good when it comes to paying royalties, and she filled us in on one or two spats with other writers."

"Are we looking at a possible motive here?" asked Reilly. "Is Vera fed up enough to do something? Does she want rid of them two so she can take over?"

"I wouldn't have thought so, Sean," said Gardener. "Even if she wanted to kill either of them, I doubt she would have been able to do what was done to Max on her own."

"She's married; her husband could have helped."

"Even so," replied Gardener, "no disrespect to females but it would have taken some physical strength to do what was done." Gardener turned to Thornton and Anderson. "Did you get the feeling she harboured more than resentment?"

"Not really," said Thornton. "She's definitely unhappy and just feels she could make a better job of it."

"It's certainly an interesting option for us," said Gardener, jotting it down on the board. "What about the spats with some of the local authors, did she give any names?"

"Yes, we got three," said Thornton. "Contacted all of them and we said we'd pop along tomorrow."

"Good work, well done. How did they sound on the phone?"

"I think disappointed would be the word, rather than bitter," said Anderson. "Seems the biggest bugbear is the royalty payments, not getting them on time and poor sales."

"That was something else Vera Purdy was annoyed about," said Thornton. "She didn't feel they promoted the books properly. It was her who would put in the extra mile. A couple of the names were big enough for signings and it was Vera who arranged those and set it up with Waterstones."

"So she felt she was doing the lion's share and seeing nothing for it?"

"Sounds that way."

"Do any of the names you were given cross-reference with anything Max had on his mobile or his laptop?" Gardener asked.

"Yes," said Anderson. "His phone confirmed quite a lot of contact, and with those names. The interesting thing was, he rarely made calls, most of them called him."

"Anybody regular in the days leading to his death?"

"Nobody that sticks out," said Thornton.

Gardener turned to Longstaff and Gates. "How do the accounts and the bank statements look?"

"Not that healthy," said Gates. "They're okay but they could probably do a lot better. They're not in debt. They do pay the bills but never on time. One of their bestsellers from what we could see was that coffee-table book you mentioned."

"Yes," said Anderson, "we had a browse through that while we were there. Did you know that they had written it?"

"Max and Cyril?" asked Reilly.

"Yes, they were down as the authors."

"Can't say as I noticed," said Reilly. "I thought it was well put together, so maybe they do know what they're doing."

"Actually," said Longstaff, "Sarah and I were looking into that very thing earlier today. Seems there *is* a dispute about who the true author is. It's going to court."

"You're kidding," said Reilly, "so they didn't write it but said they did?"

"That's what the court case is all about," said Gates. "Plagiarism."

"Who is the true author?" asked Gardener.

"You're going to like this," said Gates.

Gardener didn't say anything, simply waited for Gates to part with the information.

"Only Adi Giles."

Gardener's jaw dropped. "We're talking about the same man who found Max dead in the abbey?"

"Yes. We have the name of his solicitor who is handling the case," said Longstaff. "We gave him a quick call just to verify it and made an appointment to see him tomorrow."

"You're right," said Gardener, "we do like it."

"What we're *not* keen on," said Reilly, "is why he never mentioned it. And I'll tell you something else for nothing, he has a camper van, so he has, that could have been used as a van, and we're looking for a van."

"We'll find out why tomorrow, Sean. He's first on our list of visits." Gardener turned to Anderson and Thornton. "Did Vera Purdy mention the name of the author?"

"No, she didn't," said Thornton.

"Do you want us back there tomorrow?" asked Anderson.

"No," said Gardener, "her and Cyril are second on our list."

Gardener turned to the whiteboard, and under the heading 'suspects', he wrote three names.

Cyril Knowles. Vera Purdy, and Adi Giles.

He turned back to the team. "Thank you all, and well done. Now it's time to turn up the heat."

# Chapter Fourteen

The next morning, Reilly brought the pool car to a halt outside a moderate semi on Layton Rise in Horsforth. The house had a connecting garage, outside of which an old VW camper was parked. The lawn was well kept, the garden weed free, and the paint on the exterior of the house appeared quite fresh. The area was pretty affluent. Gardener noticed a golf club at the end of the rise.

Leaving the car, Reilly asked, "How do you want to play this?"

"Let's see if he digs himself a hole. When we spoke to him at the abbey he seemed like he had the weight of the world on his shoulders. Admittedly he *had* just found Max Knowles, but it struck me that it was more than that."

"I know what you mean," said Reilly. "He looks to me like one of life's worriers."

Gardener approached the front door and rang the bell.

"We'll find out, shall we?"

Through the glass of the front door and the bay window, Gardener could hear music playing at a level that perhaps might not have been acceptable if you lived in a one-bedroom flat on a housing estate. He wasn't quite sure of the name of the song but he recognised the singer as Cher.

He rang the bell again and stepped back. As he did so, the front door opened.

"Oh, I'm sorry," said Giles. "I didn't realise anyone was at the door."

"I'm not surprised," said Reilly.

"Lucky for us you came to the door, then," said Gardener. "Are you going somewhere?"

"No," replied Giles, a little faster than Gardener would have expected.

"May we come in and talk to you?"

Giles nodded, and stood back. He was dressed in a lemon-coloured jumper, with a blue shirt and white trousers. Today's flamboyant attire was topped off with a little black French beret.

Adi Giles invited them in and closed the front door. He strutted forward, through the hall and into what Gardener took to be the kitchen.

"I see what you mean," said Reilly to Gardener.

"About what?"

"He's uptight. Did you see the way he walked into that kitchen? Like he was trying to crack a walnut between the cheeks of his arse."

"Behave yourself, Sean."

The pair walked through and joined Adi Giles. The room was completely spotless and there was literally not one thing out of place that Gardener could see. All the colours were coordinated, and all implements lined horizontally or vertically but in a straight line.

Adi Giles pulled down three cups that had been hanging from hooks underneath a cupboard and poured both officers a coffee whether they wanted it or not. He reached into a cupboard and pulled out three, two-fingered KitKats and placed them on a plate before putting them on the table along with the drinks. He took a seat, and asked Gardener and Reilly to do so too.

Gardener never even asked a question before he started.

"Look, if it's about that shoplifting incident, it was years ago. I was only twelve, I didn't know what I was doing; I was egged on by the others." He placed his head in his hands. "Oh, God, I knew this would happen, I knew you lot would come and get me. It's not as if it was a lot. I'll pay it back. It can't be much – even with interest. It was just one of those stupid schoolboy pranks."

Gardener had the feeling that if he sat here all day and let him, Adi Giles would not stop talking, nor would he run out of steam. But his partner beat him to it.

"What did you take?" Reilly asked, seriously, playing along, pulling his notebook out of his pocket.

"Is all this really necessary?"

"I won't ask you again."

"An Aztec Bar."

"An Aztec bar?" Reilly dropped his book and pen on the table. "One of those things in a purple wrapper, like a Mars bar, only better?"

"Yes, that's it." Giles' expression was one of puzzlement.

"Christ, I love them," replied Reilly. Gardener smiled. "Any idea where they sell them now?"

"No," said Giles, confused. "Why do you ask?"

"If you did," said Reilly, "I'd go and pinch one myself – might even get another one for you."

Giles had been about to take a sip of the coffee, but stopped before the cup reached his mouth. "Are you serious?"

"Of course, I love 'em. But, like you said, it's not much of a crime, is it? Anyway we're not here about that."

"Oh, God, no." Giles put his cup down. "It's more serious, isn't it? You've really caught me now, haven't you? I know I was in the gay club, I'll admit to that, but I didn't have any drugs. Maybe I did slip out of the back door..."

"Oh, Jesus," said Reilly. "If you keep talking, we'll have enough to throw the book at you. You'll go down for a ten stretch minimum, mark my words."

"We're not here about the gay club, Mr Giles," said Gardener.

"Look, who's been talking, that's all I want to know. I'll own up. That's what they always tell you on these police dramas, isn't it, own up. Admit it, the judge will go easy on you."

"It's who *hasn't* been talking that's more important to us."

"Who *hasn't* been talking?" repeated Giles. "Well, who?"

"You," said Gardener.

"Me, about what?"

"A pending court case involving Max and Cyril Knowles. Is that ringing any bells, Mr Giles?"

His face dropped. "Oh, my, God. How did you find out about that?"

"I'm sorry," said Reilly, "I thought we were asking the questions."

"It's our job, Mr Giles. Remember, you found Max Knowles at the end of a rope in Kirkstall Abbey?"

"Don't remind me."

"And don't you interrupt me," said Gardener. "It's up to us to find out who murdered Max Knowles and put him behind bars before he can do it again. One of the things we have to do is look into the victim's background and cover every avenue. During our investigation, we discovered that the Knowles brothers had published a rather large, and very unusual coffee-table book, to say the least."

"Only, another of our officers told us that there's a big dispute going on as to the actual ownership of the book," said Reilly. "Would you like to tell us your side of the story?"

Giles stared at the ceiling and Gardener thought he was going to cry. The corners of his mouth trembled and his eyes watered.

"It's not what you think."

"At the moment," said Gardener, "we're not thinking anything. We simply want an explanation of what went on. And while you're at it you can tell us what you were doing on Kirkgate on the day of the murder, outside the Knowles' office."

"Okay, okay," said Giles. "I'll admit it, those two ripped me off. I told you to watch Cyril. He's a monster. I had an idea for what I thought would make a great book. It would be something for Yorkshire Heritage, and if I made a big thing of the abbey I thought it would sell easier."

"What is the book about?"

"It concentrated on the dark side of the county's heritage. I did a lot of research into the county's historical buildings. I went to those places and took photos of where victims had been found in the past; and each photo was accompanied by small potted history about the building and what had happened there."

"Christ," said Reilly, "that's a bit dark for you, isn't it?" He'd now finished his chocolate bar and was eyeing up Gardener's. "When we met in the abbey you said you were scared stiff of the paranormal."

"I am."

"So how come you were taking all these dark photos? You must have been in those places by yourself at night."

"I wasn't," replied Giles. "I took the photos during the day and used filters to make it look dark. Anyway, to get back to the book, they actually rejected it. Told me it was no good and to take it to a more suitable publisher."

"Did you?"

"No, I was gutted."

"Why take it to them if they only publish sporting biographies?"

"That isn't all they publish. It's the mainstay of their business but Vera Purdy reckons there is a market for this stuff, and she persuaded those two to give it a go. They did one or two smaller publications before this one."

"How did you find out about it being published?" asked Gardener.

"It was on the shelf in Waterstones. Most of the photographs in the published version are slightly different. I found out afterwards that Cyril went out and re-shot them all, from different angles. Max wrote all the narrative that went with the photos, making sure it was different to mine."

"How did you feel about that?" Reilly asked.

"I didn't want to kill either of them if that's what you're asking."

"I would have done," said Reilly.

"I'm not like that, Mr Reilly, and don't say you haven't noticed because you'd be the only one that hasn't. I told you before I have to put up with quite a lot in life, name-calling to say the least."

"What *did* you do about it?" Gardener asked. "You can't simply have turned the other cheek, solicitors are involved."

"I spoke to the Society of Authors and they asked me to submit everything, and they studied it. They said it would be very difficult to prove, or to sue, but speaking to a solicitor might be an option."

"Which you obviously did, so what did he say?"

"He agreed with them, but he didn't like to see people taken advantage of so he said he would fight it on a no-win-no-fee basis. That's where I was going when you spotted me on CCTV in Kirkgate. I'll give you his name and address."

"We already have it," said Gardener. "Why didn't you tell us all this at the abbey?"

Adi Giles sighed; one of those really heavy noises that sounded like he'd actually burst.

"I didn't want to get fingered for the hanging and end up going to prison for something I didn't do. I know how you lot work; give an inch, you take a mile."

"Be serious, son," said Reilly.

"We're here to protect the public," said Gardener. "That means everybody. We wouldn't have automatically assumed you'd done it if you'd told us all of this. We'd have investigated things properly, like we are doing now. But you could have saved us a lot of time and made things a little easier for us. As a matter of practice, where were you on the night of the murder?"

"Here, at home."

"Can you prove it, son?" asked Reilly. "Last time we spoke you said your boyfriend worked nights, so he wouldn't have been here, would he?"

"No, he wasn't; it was just me." Adi Giles suddenly jumped up. "But hang on, we spoke on the phone around ten o'clock. I can show you."

"That wouldn't help, Mr Giles. It doesn't prove where you were."

"I thought you lot could triangulate calls, pin someone down to within an inch."

"We can," said Gardener, "but it's not quite that good. Okay, give us yours and Freddie's number and we'll check."

Once that was done, Gardener asked how the case with the book was progressing.

"It isn't," said Giles. "My solicitor doesn't think I have much of a case but he's going to keep trying."

"When was the last time you saw Max Knowles?"

Adi Giles reached into a drawer and pulled out a diary. He flicked through the pages.

"About three months ago, just after the book came out. I told them I'd been to Waterstones and I'd seen it and I thought what they had done was underhand and that I was going to sue. I think I went a bit overboard because I said to them that by the time I'd finished with them they'd be lucky to still have anyone on their books. That I was going to finish them."

"Can you see how that looks to us?" Reilly asked.

Giles threw his hands in the air. "I can't win, can I? You told me to tell you everything and I am doing so."

"How did they take it?" Gardener asked.

"Max didn't say anything."

"Cyril?"

"You've met him. You know what he's like. He called me all the names under the sun, said I couldn't prove anything but to go ahead and give it my best shot. He said he would bury *me* first."

"How did that make you feel?"

"It boiled my blood, I can tell you," said Giles, with an expression that could have melted an igloo. "I was so bloody mad that I picked up an inkwell on his desk and emptied it into his tea, and then told him to drink it and to crawl back under whatever stone he'd come out from."

"Bit of a temper you have there, old son," said Reilly.

"Hardly *Reservoir Dogs*, is it?" added Gardener.

Giles tightened his face up. "Oh, that's an awful film."

"Was anything else said... or done?"

Giles appeared to be holding back.

"You might as well tell us," said Gardener. "We'll find out anyway."

"Oh, God."

Gardener and Reilly waited.

"I said I would see them in hell and that I would make them pay or I would die trying. But I promise you now, officer, I don't know who killed Max, but it certainly wasn't me."

# Chapter Fifteen

Within an hour of leaving Horsforth, they were back in the centre of Leeds at the City Chambers on Kirkgate. The weather was dry and warm and the sky cloudless. Plenty of people were using the City Market, perhaps hoping to catch a bargain. The inside of the chambers was as quiet as the previous visit but they hadn't reached the top-floor offices yet.

Eventually, they walked through the open door and spotted Vera Purdy at her desk. From the other room, Cyril was ranting about authors and publishers and the relationship they *do* have, not the one everyone *thought* they should have.

"I do hope nothing else has happened," said Vera.

"That depends on how you look at it," said Gardener.

"Sounds like it has, then," she replied.

"Why didn't you tell us about the impending court case?" Gardener asked.

"Which one?"

"Jesus," said Reilly, "how many does he have?"

"About three."

"Business is booming, then," added Gardener. He strolled over to the coffee table and grabbed the large book with a photo of Kirkstall Abbey on the front. "The one involving this book."

To give her credit, Vera Purdy didn't bat an eyelid. "Hardly a court case, more a dispute."

"Not according to Adrian Giles – solicitors are involved."

"But it still hasn't gone to court, nor is it ever likely to."

"Why?" asked Reilly. "Is Cyril going to settle out of court?"

"There's nothing to settle. Giles claims he wrote the book, but those two in there don't."

"Those *two*?" asked Gardener. "You mean there's someone else involved in the business that we haven't met?"

"Slip of the tongue, officer," replied Vera Purdy. "Anyway, if that's what you've come to talk about you'd better speak to his lordship in there. It was all his idea. Whatever went on, it was down to him, not me."

Gardener found her attitude strange. A minute ago she was defending the company; now, it was all someone else's idea. If she had designs on the publishing house itself, he could understand her defence of them. She wouldn't want any court cases outstanding if she were going to make a play for the place. However, she did intimate something was going on.

"Doesn't alter the fact that no one informed us there was bad blood between you and another author. This places him in a very bad light, makes him a possible murder suspect."

Vera Purdy laughed. "Adrian Giles, capable of committing murder? He couldn't kill a song."

"He was trying pretty hard this morning," said Reilly.

"I appreciate what you're saying, officer, but he's not your man. He's not the type. He's got bigger fish to fry."

"Which means what?" asked Gardener.

"It's not my place to say, but let's just say he has enough personal issues, that probably weigh a lot heavier on his mind. But for what it's worth, I don't think he's your killer."

"So maybe it's one of the others," said Gardener. "You need to give us all the details of all the court cases you have at the moment."

"Vera?" shouted Cyril, at a level that could have punched a hole through a wall. "What's going on out there; who the hell are you talking to?"

"Is anyone in there with him?" asked Reilly. "Or is he melting the phone lines?"

"He's by himself."

Gardener didn't say anything else, he simply headed for the door. Before going through he turned to the secretary.

"A list of the names, please, for when we come back out."

She nodded but said nothing.

"What do you want?" asked Cyril, which was almost the same opening gambit as the previous visit.

"The truth would be a help," said Gardener.

"Are you suggesting I was lying to you two last time?"

"No," said Reilly, "simply being economical, which just about sums you up, Cyril, old son."

"This is harassment."

"Change the record, Mr Knowles," said Gardener, who still had the coffee-table book in his hand.

"Look..."

"Shut up, Cyril," said Reilly. "Just answer the questions we ask, truthfully, and we'll be out of this place before you know it."

Gardener slammed the book on his desk, and the dust rose like a cloud of blowflies.

Cyril coughed and waved his arms and then glanced at the book, blinking. "What about it?"

"Who wrote it?" Gardener asked.

"We did, me and Max."

"That's not what we're hearing," said Reilly.

"Well whatever you're hearing is a load of old bollocks. We wrote it fair and square."

"Write a lot of this type of book, do you?" asked Gardener. "Only we thought you were into autobiographies."

Cyril dragged a cigar from a box on his desk and sat back. He made as if to light it.

"We'd rather you didn't, if you don't mind," said Gardener.

"It's my fucking office," he shouted, jumping out of the chair. "I can do what I like in my office."

"Not when it's our health at stake," said Gardener.

"And it's at risk just sitting here, believe me," added Reilly, glancing around.

"What are you trying say?"

"I doubt it would sink in if we told you," retorted Gardener. "Why didn't you mention the court case involving this book?"

"Court case?" shouted Cyril, sitting back down. "Don't make me laugh. It'll not go to court. Anyway, you'll have more ongoing court cases than me..."

"That's doubtful," interrupted Reilly.

"As I was about to say, you'll have more than me, do you tell me about all of yours?" Cyril threw the cigar at the window. Judging by the mess, Gardener figured he was unlikely to ever find that again.

"Adrian Giles tells a different story."

"Giles," shouted Cyril, jumping out of his seat again, his blood pressure probably almost doubling. "That nancy boy. He couldn't knock the skin off a rice pudding. You're barking up the wrong tree there... or he is."

"That's rather an insensitive comment," said Reilly, "almost prejudiced."

"It's a free country. I'm entitled to my opinion," added Cyril. "Men are men where I come from. We work down mines – play rugby at weekends."

"Is publishing a man's game?" asked Reilly.

"I haven't always been a publisher," said Cyril, sitting back down. "Vera," he shouted. "What does a man have to do to get a drink round here? The inside of my mouth's like the Gobi fucking desert."

"It's definitely the same size," muttered Reilly.

"You say something?" asked Cyril.

"I said, what about trying them for size," countered Reilly, glancing at the tea-making facilities. "You could try using them on that cabinet there."

"That's women's work."

Gardener found Cyril Knowles more revolting by the minute.

The phone rang. Cyril ignored it, instead, he began shouting for Vera again. And then he continued with his answers without blinking an eye.

"Contact sports me, all my life, that's my game. Used to be involved in wrestling."

"Oh, Christ," said Reilly, "not that again. They're not sportsmen, they're actors."

Gardener found the comment worrying. The subject had come up a number of times and there was still the matter of the mask that the flasher wore. Although they didn't think Cyril had killed Max Knowles, Gardener had a feeling the mask was going to play a part somewhere. And it still planted Cyril firmly in one of the suspect's seats.

"Tell that to them," replied Cyril. "It's a contact sport and people still get hurt."

Vera slipped in with Cyril's drink. "Would you two like a cup?"

"No, we're fine, thanks," said Gardener. "Just the list if you have it?"

"I do, it's on my desk."

"What list?" asked Cyril. "What the hell are you talking about? Don't go telling them all our business."

"Someone's killed your brother, Mr Knowles," said Gardener, "and that makes it our business. But let's get back to the book, shall we? What happened with this publication that is going to end up in court, which has almost certainly made you some enemies?"

"You'd have to ask Max that one."

"Guess that's another séance to arrange," said Reilly.

"What do you mean?" asked Gardener.

"It was nothing to do with me," retorted Cyril. "All of that," he shouted, pointing to the book, "was his idea. And hers." He pointed to Vera as she left.

Vera turned, venomously. "Don't lay all the blame on me. I'm trying to take your publishing house in a better direction."

Cyril rolled his eyes. "What do you know?"

Vera was about to jump back but Gardener stopped her. "Can we leave this for another time, please?"

"Yes," shouted Cyril, "another time, if you want to keep your job."

Vera simply left, with a disgusted expression.

"Now, where was I?" asked Cyril.

"You were carrying out a character assassination on your brother," said Reilly.

"Yes," said Cyril, as if it was the most natural thing in the world. "He took the photos, not me. He did the write-ups. I told him it was all bollocks, it would never sell."

"Seems like the sales figures are proving you wrong, Mr Knowles."

"Beginner's luck."

"Maybe," said Gardener, "but the main purpose for our visit is not entirely down to the court case..."

"Could have fooled me," interrupted Cyril.

Gardener slammed his hand on the top of the book. "We're here to find out if there's anything else you're not telling us about your brother."

"No, there isn't. And instead of coming round here hounding me, shouldn't you be out there looking for the killer?"

"That's what we're trying to do," said Reilly, "but there's a serious lack of cooperation from you."

"And very little information to actually help us," added Gardener. "We're not hounding you, Mr Knowles, we're actually trying to protect you."

"How do you make that one out?"

"Think about it," said Reilly. "With Max out of the way, it's always possible you're next!"

# Chapter Sixteen

The theatre was a wonderful place, a building where Mantra felt completely at home. When it came to shows featuring hypnotists, the audience flocked for a number of reasons: they wanted to see if they could outwit him; or to see if they could resist the spell. Most importantly, they came to watch others make fools of themselves.

When it came to illusions, that was a different ball game altogether. Most were mesmerised by what was happening. Some wondered if it was possible to spot the sleight of hand methods the illusionist actually used. Others would try to trap you outside and ask you to reveal your methods, or maybe teach them a trick to impress their friends or work colleagues.

Despite all that, the theatre was still a magical place, for both audience and performers.

He was back on stage at the City Varieties in Leeds, having completed the first half of the show with a number of willing participants that he *had* managed to hypnotise. He rarely made people appear stupid, dancing around the stage like a chicken, unless they were particularly obnoxious toward him.

Act two was all about illusions. He'd started easily, with all the usual card tricks, allowing someone to pick a card and then guessing which one it was; making them appear in different places on people's body, or even inside their phones.

He'd had someone on the stage, wrapped up his prized Omega watch in a cloth, and smashed the life out of it with a hammer. That was often hilarious, almost impossible to describe the expression, and the fear running through the person's mind; the most prominent being why the hell did I even come up here in the first place, let alone allow him to smash my watch to smithereens? The expression of relief when the watch was handed back to them in one perfect piece was priceless.

Pulling the rabbit out of the hat trick was always a winner. He'd had trouble in the past from animal rights activists but no matter how much he had tried he could never assure them that the rabbits were never hurt, or put under any stress. He wouldn't have performed the trick if they had been. He'd always maintained the highest standards and made sure the animals were treated as well as one would treat a family member.

As the evening wore on, he ramped up the tension by treating the audience to the Chinese water torture cell. It should really have been the finale because it was one that would always leave the audience gasping.

The famous Hungarian-American magician Harry Houdini first performed the escape illusion in 1912 in Berlin, Germany.

It consisted of three parts: firstly, the magician's feet were locked in stocks; he was then suspended in mid-air, from his ankles with a restraint brace; finally, he was lowered into a glass tank overflowing with water. The restraint was locked to the top of the cell.

The trick was very risky, and Mantra knew you had to be in pretty good shape to pull it off. Hanging upside down with the blood rushing to your head, while fully immersed under water for three minutes was dangerous.

He'd always survived and people constantly asked how it was done. Like he was going to tell them. Why would he? Did they want to try the trick at home? He wouldn't put it past some of them.

After finally disappearing from the stage to dry himself off and replace his face mask, Mantra slipped back out of his dressing room for the final illusion of the night. He was pleased with the way the show had gone, especially as it was becoming more difficult to pull an audience in these days, for the kind of show he did. He still had full houses but the theatres were smaller, and the ticket prices were cheaper, therefore his cut was far less than he had been used to. But he still loved it.

The applause that met him when he returned said it all.

"Thank you."

Once it had died down he spoke to them again.

"I want to thank you all for coming tonight. If you've enjoyed the show, my name is Mantra. If you haven't, it's David Copperfield."

That always raised a laugh.

"For my final illusion I would like to treat you to something completely different. Something spectacular, something that will have you talking long after you've left the building."

He had them already. Most of them were probably thinking they'd seen everything.

"I'd like to take you back to the turn of the twentieth century."

The lights dimmed and a strange eerie piece of music reverberated quietly around the room. Eventually there was no lighting on the stage, and only one spot on Mantra. He wanted the audience concentrating on him, and him alone.

"The first steel and concrete stage ever built in Hollywood was made for the film, *The Phantom of the Opera*.

It housed the entire interior set of the Opera House, as well as the backstage area and the grand staircase, and still stands today on the Universal Studios Lot, known as Stage 28."

He heard the odd gasp from the theatre.

Mantra continued. "Joseph Buquet is a fictional character in *The Phantom of the Opera*, a novel written in 1910 by the author Gaston Leroux. Joseph is the chief stagehand for the theatre, who claims to have seen the Opera Ghost.

"In the novel he is one of the first to see the phantom, Erik, describing him as 'extraordinarily thin, with his dress coat hanging from his frame. His eyes are so deep that you can hardly see the fixed pupils; just two big black holes, as in a dead man's skull. His skin is stretched across his bones like a drumhead, and not white, but a pasty yellow. His nose is so little worth talking about that you cannot see it side face, and the absence of the nose is a horrible thing to look at. All the hair he has is three or four dark locks on his forehead and behind his ears'."

The stage lighting changed. A screen behind Mantra was backlit from a projector, allowing the audience a view of the Opera House, but still not enough to see much of the stage itself.

"Joseph is found hanged," said Mantra, building the tension, "in the third cellar between a flat and a set piece from *Le roi de Lahore*, right next to the entrance to the phantom's torture chamber."

More areas of the stage were now being eerily lit, and a thin mist drifted across the whole area.

The sound from the lapel microphone that Mantra wore changed, as more echo had been added.

"In the stage production, if the noose in the Final Lair scene doesn't function correctly, the actor knows to back up and throw himself against the portcullis, as if it's electrically charged, and has a magnetic pull holding him back against the grid. We always want the noose to work."

Above him, the audience attention was drawn to a banging noise. Mantra glanced upwards. He could almost feel the tension, the anticipation at the thought of what they were going to witness.

"Ladies and gentlemen, what you are about to see is a recreation of that Final Lair scene from *The Phantom of the Opera*. This stunt is extremely difficult to pull off even by someone who is trained in stunts/stage combat. I must impress that you never try anything like this at home."

He always said that but he suspected some of them would.

The stage lighting increased slightly, and the view of the Opera House on the back screen disappeared, replaced by something that resembled a cell with plain grey walls, a blanked-out window frame, and a large trapdoor in the floor that had been lifted. A light projected up through the gap.

Further banging noises came from the rafters above the stage, followed by a metallic clang, as if metal had struck metal. Urgent, whispering voices could also be heard. Mantra stepped back and to one side, allowing the audience a full view of the stage. He glanced upwards, showing concern, but he never said anything.

Further noises emanated around the theatre and it started to sound like a scuffle had started from up above. Dull, thudding sounds. The audience gasped and the concern became evident as more than one – especially the females – brought hands to their mouth.

"Careful," shouted a voice from above.

Mantra leaned forward, peering toward the roof trusses, unable to see too much because of the position of the spotlights.

As he moved to his right to try to gain a better view, everything happened at once.

"Watch out!" shouted a voice.

But whatever he was referring to, there was no time. A sudden whooshing sound, followed by a whiplash of some description brought the whole thing to a sudden halt as a body – dressed in blue – fell the full length, straight through the trapdoor.

The women screamed, the men gasped and the stagehand shouted: "Jesus Christ!"

Mantra moved to one side very quickly. The body on the rope was struggling intently, whipping around like a snake. There was obviously a struggle of some kind going on and it appeared that everyone connected to the production was powerless to help.

Mantra tried to grab the rope but he didn't have the strength to control it. He glanced upwards, before finally glaring at the side of the stage.

"Cut!" he shouted, his voice sounding like a chainsaw. "Curtains, please, and lights."

The last the audience saw of anything was Mantra desperately trying to lift the rope. The curtains closed and the music cut, leaving only agitated voices. The lights blacked out altogether. A safety precaution to keep the audience in place for the time being.

Eventually, the agitated voices on the stage ceased and the whole place fell into silence.

After what appeared to be an eternity, the lights came back on and the curtains had been opened but there was no one on the stage. The rope was still hanging through the trapdoor, but now, it was motionless.

The sudden sound of a hundred voices rose through the small auditorium, as no one had any idea what was going on. Questions flew round at top speed.

"What's happened?"

"Who was on the end of the rope?"

"Is he dead?"

"Well if he isn't he'll probably wish he was," shouted someone else.

People glanced around all over the place. "Where is the magician?"

Finally, a slow hand clap began to silence them, and Mantra appeared from the back of the building. "Thank you, ladies and gentlemen." He stopped clapping. "Thank you all for coming and taking part in the show. I hope you all enjoyed what you saw and, please, have a safe journey home."

People were still not leaving. The confusion within the building was contagious.

"Oh, I almost forgot," said Mantra. "Would you all please help me to say a huge thank you to our actor this evening. I like to call him the fall guy."

The man dressed all in blue suddenly appeared from behind a curtain and took a bow.

"A guaranteed showstopper, I think you'll all agree."

The man in blue took his bow, obviously appreciating the rapturous applause.

# Chapter Seventeen

As the clock in the corner of the room struck eleven, Cyril peered at it, but it was only for the fact that he heard eleven chimes that he actually knew what time it was. He decided that whatever the hour, it was time to pour another. Reaching down into the cupboard section of his desk, he drew out the bottle of Famous Grouse, single malt, which he kept for special occasions. You can keep all the other shit, thought Cyril; Grouse topped them all. And who was he kidding, special occasion? Any occasion will do as an excuse for a drink.

After he'd poured two very generous fingers worth, he screwed the cap back on and placed the bottle in the cupboard, staring out of the window. That was a pointless task, he was four floors up so he couldn't see anything.

He sat back, thinking about Max, and their differences. There were many but the partnership had always worked. They'd pulled a few late nights in the office. Cyril chuckled when he thought about those. Fuck all was ever achieved.

Vera usually left at five and he and Max would soldier on – as they called it – till around seven; seven thirty some nights. But then, whatever was going on, it stopped. The drinks came out, followed by the menus. Max liked Chinese. Cyril always preferred Indian. The takeaways were next door to each other, and the drivers had grown accustomed to the choices. Whichever one was nearest the office would bring both meals.

Cyril laughed out loud, thinking back to the time the pair of them went way over the top, finishing a bottle of whisky in one night. Vera turned up the next morning, found the heating on full, the empty bottle, and the pair of them asleep across the desk. She claimed the place smelled like a Thai brothel; though how the fuck she knew, Cyril had no idea. She'd never left Yorkshire.

Max and Cyril had. A favourite haunt was Blackpool. Christ, they'd had some benders in that place.

Max was always the ideas man, time and again coming up with a new direction in which to take the business. Cyril was the money-man – it was usually his job to finance it all. Though why, he didn't know. Max had clearly been far better with the money, if you considered how well he approached his little gambling ventures. He rarely lost and if he did it didn't make much difference because it all came out of the jar.

Max's big mistake was that he thought Cyril had been as good, and as cautious. And it *was* a big mistake. Cyril was definitely watertight. Of that there was no doubt. But he had to be. When they were kids they had no money, which pretty much continued throughout their lives. What Max had, he saved. What Cyril had, he blew. He'd also managed to wheedle his way into the company bank accounts and he'd led Max to believe they were doing okay.

Fat chance.

Cyril felt one of his headaches coming on and reached down into the same cupboard as the whisky. He found a couple of out-of-date painkillers and he knew you shouldn't mix them with alcohol; and that was when they were in date. Fuck knows what would happen to him out of date. Still, he threw them into his cakehole and swilled them down with the firewater.

He also came across an out-of-date Cornish pasty from Greggs. What the hell, it was better than nothing.

Once he'd polished it off, along with a chocolate bar he'd also found – but that was in date – he glanced at the files in front of him.

Most if not all of the day he'd been trying to figure out who had killed his brother, and why. The words of the policemen were also branded into his brain, the fact that he could be next. Who had they managed to upset to such a degree?

Maybe *they* hadn't. Maybe it was only Max. But Cyril knew that would not be true. *He* was by far the more aggressive of the two.

He picked up the first file. Vera had left them on his desk before she went home. They were the up-and-coming court cases, or disputes as he preferred to call them.

Hunslet Printers were suing them for an unpaid bill. It was a bit more than that. The invoice had been outstanding for two years, and quite how Cyril had managed to swerve it he wasn't sure. One thing he *was* sure about, Max hadn't known anything about it.

It had happened because Cyril had taken a huge gamble on an ex-wrestler from Yorkshire, Barry Roberts, aka the Wakefield Warrior, who had decided to write his autobiography. For Cyril, it was a guaranteed winner. The man had been massive. Fought all over the world, made his living in places like Japan, India, America; everywhere there was money to be made, he made it.

But that was the problem. No one in the UK had known Roberts. He'd never been on the TV in the golden years. Cyril told the printer it would be huge, ordered a print run of five thousand books. He informed them that they would most likely sell out within a week, guaranteeing more sales. He had personally – using Vera's help – set up a number of signings in the Waterstones shops throughout Yorkshire.

Nothing happened. They were lucky if five people a night had attended. He ended up massively out of pocket and he still had four thousand five hundred of the bastards in a lock-up, if the mice hadn't eaten them. The printers had been chasing the money ever since. Come to think of it, so had Barry Roberts.

But surely neither party would kill Max over a few lousy quid. Last Cyril had heard, Barry Roberts had knees and elbows the size of cabbages that rattled and clicked more than a tin of nuts and bolts. It couldn't possibly be him. Nor was it likely to be the printer. That's why they were heading to court.

Cyril took a swig of whisky and threw the file into the corner of the room, where it hit the clock and the pair of them landed up on the floor.

The next file was an ex-Leeds United player who was suing for non-payment of royalties. To be fair the book hadn't been a bad seller but so far it had only broken even. He couldn't pay what it hadn't made. Try telling that to the player.

"Christ," said Cyril, "this is fucking pointless." That file also ended up in a heap in the corner.

It was all small fry. People didn't kill for small fry. Whoever had taken Max, either had the wrong man, or it was something far more serious. And if they were going to take it out on one of them then why hadn't they killed Cyril? He was the bigger bastard, and he knew it.

But had Max been up to no good, with something that Cyril knew nothing about?

"No way," murmured Cyril, into his glass.

Another file on the desk was for unpaid rent on the building, but to be fair he could rule that one out. They were always behind with the rent but the landlord was a bigger fucking rogue than Cyril. He'd been up to all sorts of dodgy deals, and Cyril ought to know because he'd been involved in a few. No, Cyril had far more on the landlord that could land *him* in much deeper water, so it was very unlikely he had been involved.

Cyril didn't bother throwing that file. He slid it off the desk instead, where it landed on top of an overflowing wastepaper bin.

Cyril then noticed another file – one he hadn't seen before. Who did that belong to? Was some other poor fucker wasting his time, chasing down money they would never receive?

Glancing at his glass, Cyril noticed it was empty. *When had he finished that?* He couldn't remember drinking *any* of it, let alone all of it.

"Fucking hell," said Cyril, "has it got to that stage?"

He reached into the cupboard, unscrewed the cap and poured the remainder of the whisky, which amounted to two more fingers. Something else he would have to find the money for. Still, Vera could always chalk it up to expenses, he laughed.

Then it struck him. Vera. Was Vera responsible for Max's demise? Cyril snorted. Not a chance. If it had been Cyril himself, he could understand it. She didn't like him. Gave him all sorts of grief; often brought back the wrong food from Greggs, or forgot to pick up his painkillers for these bastard headaches that were becoming all too frequent. He was convinced it was her fucking nagging that caused them. God knows what her husband saw in her.

But no, it couldn't be Vera. Not even if she was in league with someone. Cyril went into fits of laughter when he thought maybe Vera was in league with that blond-haired ponce from Horsforth, Giles. Not a chance. Vera was more of a man than he was.

"Fuck it," shouted Cyril, slamming his glass on the desk. Some of the whisky slopped onto the file and he quickly wiped it off and opened it.

The picture and the name staring back at him nearly caused his head to implode.

"And you can fuck off as well. There's no way you'll get a penny out of me."

The files landed in a heap with the others.

A noise in the outer office – Vera's office – suddenly startled Cyril. The hinges on the door had definitely squeaked.

"Who the hell is this?" He stared at his watch but then realised he wasn't wearing it. He peered at the clock but then he remembered it was on the floor.

In a fit of rage, Cyril stood on wobbly legs and made his way unsteadily to the door.

He opened it quickly, hoping to give whoever it was a bit of a shock.

But it was Cyril who received the shock as the figure in the shadows loomed forward.

"What the hell are you doing here?"

# Chapter Eighteen

"Jesus Christ!" said Sean Reilly. "Whoever this is, knows how to pick a location."

Gardener and Reilly were on Kirkgate in the centre of Leeds. It was seven o'clock in the morning. The clouds overhead were dark grey, the rain had been steadily falling through most of the night, and from what Gardener could see he doubted that much of the scene hadn't been contaminated.

They were staring at the body of Cyril Knowles. Like his brother, his head was in a noose at the end of a rope, which had started somewhere in his office. He'd obviously gone through the grimy window that Gardener didn't think had ever been opened, and was now dangling two floors down, in front of the accountant's window. That would be a lovely start to their working day. It isn't exactly the best start to ours, either, thought Gardener.

Cyril had been spotted by a market trader on his way to work. He'd called it in about an hour ago. After hearing what had happened, Gardener immediately called the rest of the team, the pathologist, the SOCOs, and anyone else he could think of so hopefully, he wouldn't have too long a wait before he could start closing things down.

The market trader was standing inside the market entrance, dressed in a black tee shirt and jeans, with a black quilted jacket and trainers on, his expression almost as grey as his hair. They had yet to take a statement, but the man wasn't going anywhere.

"Sean, can you pop into the market and see if anyone has an extendable ladder? We need to get up there and just confirm a few things."

Reilly turned and entered the market, speaking to the trader who'd discovered the body. He scratched his head and they both disappeared inside. Gardener wondered why people scratched their head when you asked them a question they didn't know the answer to. Did it help? Ten minutes later, three people, including Reilly emerged from the market with a ladder big enough to put Gardener on the roof if he so wished – which he didn't.

"That was a stroke of luck," said Reilly, "the bloke who found him runs a shop in there and he only had this delivered yesterday, for a customer."

"Pity he didn't sell it yesterday," said Gardener, "we might have had a possible suspect."

Reilly laughed. "I thought I was the one who did the grave humour."

"See, you're a bad influence," replied Gardener, "that's what working with you does. It rubs off on me. Anyway, you have enough to contend with."

Three squad cars appeared and Gardener's team emerged.

"What in God's name?" said Bob Anderson, approaching the building.

"This just gets worse," said Frank Thornton. "What the hell does this bloke do for an encore?"

Gardener asked Reilly to position the ladder and then turned to speak to the team.

"Okay, just give me a few minutes to go up there and find out what I can, then I think we can issue a few actions."

"This must have started on the inside?" said Julie Longstaff.

"I would think so," said Gardener. "Luckily for us no one inside the building has started work yet, and they're not likely to for a couple of hours, which gives us a bit of time to play with."

Gardener turned, buttoned up a large, padded jacket and approached the ladder.

"Do you want me to go, boss?"

"No, it's okay, Sean. It's not that far up."

"Maybe not, but it's wet, so watch your footing."

Gardener tested the ladder. As he climbed up, Reilly and Sharp stood either side and held on to it. As he drew level with Cyril Knowles, the first thing that hit him was the smell. Cyril had soiled himself, which indicated it was the probably the hanging that killed him.

Gardener took two or three more steps. He glanced down and wished he hadn't. It was higher than he'd thought and now, of all times, he could feel the flexing of the ladder. Until he'd glanced at the ground, he hadn't given it another thought.

He stared at Cyril's face. His complexion was ash grey, and his eyes were still open. Gardener leaned in a little closer and could not detect any of the little red dots known as petechiae that had been evident in Max; another sign that he had not been strangled. Stupidly, but necessarily, Gardener reached out with one hand and felt Cyril's cold and clammy wrist for a pulse. There was nothing.

Peering at the rope, the hangman's noose was tied perfectly. Gardener peered more closely at Cyril's head. The rope was underneath the chin and tight up behind the ears. There were no marks on or around the throat; a further indication that he'd been killed by hanging rather than strangled and then hung like his brother.

There was very little else he could do so he descended the ladder. As he reached ground level, the Home Office pathologist appeared at his side. "What were you doing up there?"

"Checking the cladding," said Gardener.

"What kind of a stupid question was that?" asked Reilly. He turned to his partner. "But I like the answer, you're definitely getting more like me."

"God forbid," said Fitz, "one of you is more than enough for any team."

"Seeing as you weren't here I had to check for myself that he was dead."

"You don't think I'm going up there, do you?" asked Fitz, his expression as grave as his profession.

"It's your job, isn't it?" asked Reilly.

Fitz didn't reply, simply gave Reilly his most fearsome scowl. He turned to Gardener. "Foul play?"

"Definitely. And for the record, he is dead. There's no pulse, and his colour is awful. He's soiled himself."

Gardener turned to Reilly. "Okay, let's get things moving." He gestured for the team to come forward. "He's obviously been killed where he's landed so we'll have to drop a cordon around here, build a tent around him, have him photographed and once we've done that we can let him down for Fitz to make a quick examination before taking him to the morgue."

The rain started to fall a little harder, which Gardener didn't appreciate; neither would the team.

"Sean and I will go up into the office and see what we can find there. Can someone call Vera Purdy, let her know what's happened, and ask her if she can come down here? It's possible there may be something amiss in the office that she might spot, which would save us a bit of time.

"I'd also like a statement from the man who found him." Gardener turned to Reilly. "What's his name?"

"George Harrison, believe it or not." Reilly then addressed the team. "He runs a place in the market called Harrison's, sells all sort of DIY stuff. I've left him sitting on a seat outside his shop, drinking a strong black coffee."

"Okay," said Gardener. "Julie, Sarah, can you two pull up the CCTV from the camera facing this area? There must be something on there that will help. We'll need to interview all the people who run a business inside this building, those across the street, and probably everyone in the City Market."

"Are we closing it down?" asked Rawson.

Gardener thought about it, and then said: "I can't see any point in that. Whatever happened to Cyril Knowles must have been in the early hours of the morning, so I doubt anyone from any of these businesses was working when that happened."

"Which once again means nobody will have seen anything," added Anderson.

"Hopefully it won't matter," said Sarah Gates. "We should have a field day with the CCTV." She turned and stared at the wall opposite, quickly locating it. "There it is."

"Once again, boss," said Rawson, "whoever did this, they're bloody confident. They know the area, and they know the Knowles brothers."

"I agree, Dave," said Gardener. "For me it also backs up the theory that whoever is responsible, Cyril and Max will have known them. Hopefully, for us, their killer has been *too* confident and slipped up somewhere along the line."

Longstaff turned and glanced at the camera. "And unlike the one at the abbey, that doesn't look as if it's been moved."

A couple of vans appeared on Kirkgate, mounting the pavement and parking in front of the market entrance. A team of SOCOs exited the van.

Steve Fenton approached and studied Cyril's hanging body. "Jesus," was all he said.

Gardener issued instructions and then set his team to work. He and Reilly suited and booted and then climbed the stairs to the top floor office. Like each visit they had previously made, the door was open.

The pair walked in and as far as Gardener could ascertain, nothing in Vera's office was out of place. The chair was placed neatly underneath the desk. Her computer and monitor didn't appear to have moved. The tea-making facilities were still on the cabinet. There was no sign of a struggle.

Gardener peered down, studying the floor. He noticed that the carpet was more a large rug covering most of the room, leaving a border of floorboards. Rather than walk across the carpet, he edged his way to Cyril's door and stepped cautiously in.

"Looks like a bomb's hit the place," said Gardener.

"How can you tell?"

Gardener smiled. There was definitely evidence of a scuffle. He noticed the brass clock on the floor in one corner. The two chairs in front of the desk had been moved, one was on its side. The desk itself had been cleared but sitting neatly on top, in the middle, were three files.

Behind the desk, Gardener noticed a large black fireplace. He hadn't really clocked it on the previous visits but mainly because Cyril had been sat in front of it. On top of the fireplace he noticed a pile of envelopes standing behind a carriage clock.

He edged his way round and nearer to the mantelpiece. He saw a packet of sweeteners, and a box of Tic Tacs at one end; at the other, a model of the Blackpool Tower. Gardener felt it was out of place because it was new. Nothing else was. He felt sure he would have noticed it previously. Maybe someone had bought it for him.

He glanced at the desk. The cupboard door was open, with an empty bottle of Grouse inside. The empty glass was on top of the desk, next to the files.

"Can't fault his taste in whisky," said Reilly.

"About the only thing he probably did have any taste in," replied Gardener.

By far the most disturbing piece of evidence was the smashed window with the rope going through it. The other end had been lashed to the filing cabinet, which appeared to have gone forward with what little weight Cyril carried, but had then wedged up against the desk.

"Do you think he smashed it going through it?" Gardener asked Reilly. "Or was it smashed to make an easier exit?"

"I doubt whoever did this wanted to make life easy for him," said Reilly. "Maybe Cyril smashed it in an effort to try and escape."

"Must have been pretty desperate, we're four floors up."

"You're probably right," said Reilly. "No matter how bad things were, I doubt you'd choose that as an exit."

"He'd soiled himself," said Gardener, "so after what had happened to his brother, I would wager this is not suicide."

Reilly glanced at the files. "Let's see, shall we?"

The first one they opened belonged to a printer called Hunslet Printers.

"Interesting," said Gardener, "these refer to the possible court cases that Vera gave us yesterday. Hunslet Printers are chasing an unpaid bill. We'd best have someone round there today."

Another file revealed the name of an ex-Leeds United footballer, Duncan Preston, suing for unpaid royalties. The third referred to the landlord of the building.

"Dodgy Danny Drake," said Reilly. "Christ, no wonder Cyril threw himself out of the window if that snake owns the building."

Gardener laughed. "Not his style, though, is it, Sean. Danny Drake might lean on Cyril a bit for his money but he's not likely to want to draw attention to himself with what *he* gets up to. But still, that's two more people to hunt down and see what they know."

Gardener's mobile chimed. Steve Fenton was calling him to inform him that Vera Purdy had arrived. As they had not yet covered the scene with the tent, he said she was justifiably upset.

The pair of them left the office and found her outside the building in tears "Oh my God," she said, "who would do such a thing?"

Gardener placed an arm around her shoulder and led her toward the City Market.

"Sean, can you take her to one of the cafes and order drinks while I have a word with the SOCOs?"

He thought about asking them to sweep the office but he really preferred that Vera Purdy see it first, and point out if there was anything alien to the scene that she could tell them about.

He glanced around Kirkgate. Crime Scene tape covered that entrance of the market but there were other entrances for people to use. The outer cordon reached all the way to the edge of the road. He saw two of his officers conducting interviews with people arriving who were opening their shops on the opposite side of the road. And it was still raining.

Ten minutes later, after depositing the scene suit in a bin, he found Vera and Reilly, and also a hot cup of tea waiting for him.

He edged his way onto the bench seat. Vera had wiped her eyes but her mascara had run and mingled with the rest of her face paint, to the point she now resembled a zebra, but he doubted she cared.

"Are you okay, Mrs Purdy?"

"After seeing that? What do you think?"

"I realise it must have been a shock but we need to ask you a few questions."

"Could you not have asked them at home, where I live?" she sipped more tea.

"If it had just been questions, yes, we could have done."

"Why? What else is there?"

"Once we've finished here, we'd like to escort you carefully into the office and help us with the scene."

Vera's expression would have frozen a hot chip pan. "What, you want me to go back in there and clean the bloody place up?"

"No, Vera, love," said Reilly. "You'd need *Rentokil* for Cyril's office."

"No," added Gardener, "we want you to have a look around and tell us if everything in there *should* be in there: is there anything missing, or has anything been added."

"Hardly likely to tell with his pit."

Gardener figured that she hadn't lost her sense of humour. "How was Cyril yesterday?"

"Same as any other day," she replied. "Grumpy. Thought nowt of upsetting folk. Bad mouthed everyone, including his brother."

"Did he take any phone calls that got heated?"

"They all got heated by the time he'd finished; nothing special that I can remember. I ran a few errands for him, picked up the usual: junk food, and tablets for his headaches. He's been having a few of them lately."

"He won't be getting any more," said Reilly.

"What time did you leave the office yesterday?" Gardener asked.

"Actually I left early, about four o'clock."

"Where was he?" asked Reilly.

"Sitting at his desk, filling his face. He had a sandwich, and I made him a cup of tea. He was grumbling, as usual." She glanced up at Gardener, her eyes imploring him. "I know we didn't get on, and I didn't really like him, more for the way he treated people rather than owt else, but I wouldn't wish this on him at all."

She placed her face in her hands. "What a bloody awful way to go; and so public. Who could have done such a thing?"

She suddenly stopped talking and her expression darkened.

"What's wrong?" asked Gardener.

"I was just thinking. If them two have gone, what if I'm next? Is someone trying to take over the business and this is the way to do it, as far as they're concerned?"

"From what we can see, Vera, love, there isn't much of a business to take over," said Reilly.

"Not now," she said, "but with the right people and the right books it could be a little gold mine."

Gardener wondered if she meant herself, but he didn't feel now was the time to pursue that angle.

"As a matter of course, where were you last night, Mrs Purdy?"

"Well, we were here, in Leeds, me and my husband. We had a rare night out. We don't often go out but last night it was his birthday and I decided to treat him to a meal out and a show."

"Where was that?"

"The meal was at Bella Italia, he loves Italian food." She suddenly fished inside her bag and pulled out the receipt, as if it was actually necessary. "And then we went to the City Varieties to see that hypnotist. Or is he a magician? I don't rightly know. He does a bit of both. But he's bloody good."

"What time did it all finish, Vera?"

She checked her watch, as if that would help in any way. "About ten, I think."

"Then what, did you drive home?"

"No, we booked a taxi from the theatre. The driver picked us up on The Headrow."

"You didn't drive around here, did you?" Gardener asked, meaning Kirkgate.

"No, he took the ring road and out to Rodley."

Pity, thought Gardener. He tried another angle of attack. "We found three files on his desk, Mrs Purdy, did you put them there?"

Her attention had been piqued, judging by her expression. "Three? No, I put them there but there were four."

"Whose files did you place on his desk?"

"Let me see." She counted them off on her fingers. "Hunslet Printers was one. They rang again yesterday."

"Did they often call?"

"Almost daily," she replied. "To be fair, they were trying to give him an easy option. Settle up, even if it were on terms, and try and keep it out of court."

"The others," pressed Reilly.

"Duncan Preston, an ex-player for Leeds. Then there was one from the landlord, Danny Drake, but to be honest he wasn't taking Cyril to court, it was just a reminder that he owed money."

"And the fourth?"

"That one was fresh. It landed yesterday, from Adrian Giles' solicitor. He reckoned it was worth Giles going to court. Felt he did have something of a case."

"What did Cyril say about that one?" Reilly asked.

"He just laughed, said they had two chances; fat chance and no chance. His very words were, 'that ponce can go and fuck right off'. Excuse my French, officer."

"That phrase is definitely not French, Vera, love," laughed Reilly. "It *was* very Cyril, though."

Gardener figured there wasn't much else she could tell them. They knew about three of the files because they had seen them. The fourth was no surprise because they knew Adi Giles had already told them he'd set that one in motion.

Big question was, why was that file missing?

"And there's something else I think you ought to know," said Vera to Gardener.

"What?"

"It's about Giles."

She had their attention now.

"What about him?" Reilly asked.

"I think all of this business with the book and the court case might have unbalanced the lad a bit."

"Why would you say that?" asked Gardener.

"Unbalanced him enough to kill?" added Reilly.

Vera Purdy scowled. "Well I don't think it's done that much harm to him. But that hypnotist I went to see last night, I believe he does private sessions, to help people, like."

"And you think he's treating Adrian Giles?"

"I have it on good authority Giles has been receiving therapy from this Mantra bloke – that's his name, Mantra."

"How do you know?"

"Because my sister also goes for similar therapy. Last time she was there I went and picked her up and I saw Adrian Giles sitting in the waiting area."

Interesting, thought Gardener. But then she took the wind out of his sails.

"And Giles was there last night as well, at the show. I saw him in the audience."

# Chapter Nineteen

Ronnie Robinson parked his car in the canal car park, on Calverley Bridge in Rodley. He switched off the engine, stayed in his seat, staring out at the water. The rain had finally stopped, and as the afternoon wore on the sun had made an appearance. It was now quite pleasant. Which was more than could be said for Ronnie.

Before stepping out of the car he glanced once again at the letter he had been sent by the benefits people. He'd had to ask his neighbour about that one; you had to be a Bletchley codebreaker to understand a council letter. The gist of the correspondence said that he was being investigated, and his benefits were being stopped until they ascertained whether or not the claim that he was working and cheating the benefit people was true.

Ronnie was seething, not to mention desperate. Without money – and everything that came with it: the car, the house, and any other advantages – he hadn't a hope in hell of any kind of life.

Who the hell had made the complaint?

Ronnie suddenly wondered if it was the person he was here to meet. They'd had a short but slightly heated conversation on the phone two or three days previously. Ronnie had spent the afternoon staring at the business card he'd found at the abbey, debating whether or not to call him.

He stepped out of the car, locked it, and scurried across to The Railway Inn, the pre-arranged meeting place. The pub was large, and in a picturesque setting opposite the

Leeds/Liverpool Canal. Half a dozen cars were in the car park, and Ronnie suddenly started to wonder if he had bitten off more than he could chew. Had it really been a good idea? If the man really was a killer, Ronnie might never be seen again.

He glanced at the business card again. He called the number but hung up after the first ring, when he heard it in the distance.

Adi Giles was standing next to a battered VW camper van, dressed in black leather trousers, a pink shirt, white jacket, and a black French beret. He'd been filing his nails, as if he hadn't a care in the world. He'd jumped out of his skin when his phone rang. Ronnie now decided it might be easier than he thought. In fact, it might actually be a piece of cake.

He approached Giles, as his own phone suddenly rang. Giles glanced up and Ronnie cursed inwardly as he had forgotten to prefix the number with 141, which had now given the game away.

"Who the hell are you?" asked Giles. "What do you want? Why are you bothering me? What have I ever done to you?"

*Christ, what's he on? What's with all the fucking questions?* Ronnie had a sudden thought to play the hardman. "Never you mind who I am."

But it didn't really suit because he certainly didn't have the image, or the confidence to pull it off.

"Was it you who rang me the other day and said we needed to talk?"

"Who else would it be, dimwit?"

Giles placed his phone into his little leather bag. "Well I don't know who you are, and I've never seen you before so I can't really think what we have to talk about."

Ronnie was about to speak when Giles steamrollered on. "Is this anything to do with Freddie?"

"Who's Freddie?" asked Ronnie.

"Never you mind."

"Never mind? You asked the fucking question," shouted Ronnie.

"Are you one of those scummy little drug dealers who's always threatening Freddie? And watch your language."

"What the hell are you talking about? I don't do drugs."

"Well who are you, then? I don't have all day, and if I did I wouldn't be spending it with you. When did you last have a wash?"

"What," said Ronnie, losing his grip. "Listen, mate, I summoned you here because I said we had important business to discuss, which doesn't include my hygiene. So let's get on with it, shall we?"

Ronnie subconsciously lifted his jumper and sniffed it. *What's the cheeky bastard on about? I've only been wearing it a week and it still smells fine.*

Giles stepped back a bit. He was obviously unsure. "Yes, you mentioned the abbey."

"That's right. The abbey, you remember it."

"Be hard not to, wouldn't it, the size of it. Anyway, what have you got to say? When did you last eat?"

*Jesus Christ! More questions.* "Never mind about my fucking welfare, or whether I've eaten or not, and have I had a wash. I'll have you know I have a bath once a month whether I need it or not."

Adi Giles' eyes nearly left his head. "Once a month?"

"Look," shouted Ronnie, squeezing his hands together, "never mind all that shit. We're not here to talk about me, we're here to talk about the abbey."

"So you keep saying. Get on with it, then," said Giles. "I've told you I don't have all day."

"Not here," said Ronnie.

"Pardon?" said Giles, his eyes darting all over the place.

"I said, not here."

"That's what I thought you said." Giles took another step back. "Well, where?" He turned to his van. "Not in there, I'll have you know. It might not be the cleanest vehicle on the planet but it's cleaner than you. And I'm not going to your car, wherever that might be. Have you got a car? I doubt it, you don't even look as if you can afford a bike."

"Will you can it with the insults? It's supposed to be me interrogating you."

"Well, you're not making a very good job."

"I haven't had the fucking chance, have I?" shouted Ronnie, stamping his feet. "You haven't stopped with the personal shit since I walked over here."

"Well where, then? I haven't got all day."

"So you keep saying, but you must have some time or you wouldn't be here."

Ronnie was frustrated to fuck now, and really losing his rag.

"Go on, then," said Giles, as if everything was now Ronnie's fault. So help him God, he wasn't a violent man but he was really going to hurt Giles if he didn't play ball.

"Down there." Ronnie pointed to the towpath. "There's a bench about fifty feet down. Let's go there and talk."

Giles finally agreed but his expression said otherwise. He pulled his little bag closer, as if Ronnie was going to make off with it. Which was very unlikely. There would be fuck all in there that Ronnie wanted: probably full of lipstick, powder and paint.

Ronnie took off, quickly. Giles followed, and when they finally found the seat, he asked. "Why do you want to talk about the abbey?"

"Didn't you see me at the abbey?"

"When?"

"The other night."

"Which other night for God's sake," said Giles. "You'll have to be more precise than that."

"Tuesday."

"Tuesday?" repeated Giles, shaking his head. "I didn't see anyone on Tuesday," he protested, "because I wasn't there on Tuesday."

It wasn't going how Ronnie had imagined. "You were there all right. I saw you."

"I beg your pardon," said Giles, "I don't think you did. I was there on Wednesday morning. Maybe you're getting mixed up."

"I'm not stupid," shouted Ronnie, leaving the bench and nearly falling into the canal because he didn't see the rock at the water's edge. "I know the difference between night and day, and which day of the week it is."

"Okay, calm down."

"Calm fucking down? I'm trying to do you a favour here and all you're doing is creating problems."

"A favour?" said Giles. "You're trying to put *me* somewhere I wasn't, and you call it a favour? Do you have any proof?"

Ronnie was sideswiped. He stalled a little. "I might have."

"Might have," said Giles. "That's not very good, is it? Might have. You either have or you haven't. Oh God," Giles suddenly said, placing his immaculate fingers and nails on his face. "Why am I even doing this? I have so many things going on in my life and I'm sitting here wasting it with Worzel Gummidge."

"Worzel fucking Gummidge," shouted Ronnie, pointing his finger, but not really knowing what he would do with it. "I warned you about the insults."

"How do you know it was me," said Giles, as if he hadn't even heard Ronnie, "if you have no proof?"

"I do have proof," persisted Ronnie, sitting down, thinking that he might now have the upper hand because Giles' expression altered.

"Go on, then."

"Go on, what?" said Ronnie.

"Show me the proof. Do you have a photo?"

Oh, Jesus. Things were going awry. "Not exactly."

"Not exactly. Why?"

"How could I? Your face was covered by a bloody great camera."

"So, you don't know it was me?" said Giles, folding his arms and crossing his legs. "Exactly what proof *do* you have?"

In a fit of temper, Ronnie pulled the business card from his jacket. "Here, what's this?"

Giles took it. "My card."

"Exactly."

Giles stared at Ronnie as if his brain had suddenly started to dribble out of his ears. "What? This is it? This is your proof? Doesn't prove anything."

"It proves you were there."

"I'm not *denying* I was at the abbey, but the morning after it happened. Not before. I take it you're talking about the hanging?"

"Well, what else?"

"Could be anything with you," replied Adi Giles. "You're trying to frame me for something I haven't done. I was not at the abbey on Tuesday night taking photos. If you're insinuating what I think you are, how ghoulish would that be? Taking photos of a dead man?"

"Takes all sorts," said Ronnie.

"Evidently," said Giles, staring at Ronnie as if he was a turd. He suddenly turned the tables. "How do I know *you* didn't do it?"

"Me?"

"Yes, you."

"I didn't," protested Ronnie.

"I've only your word for that," said Giles. "How do I know you didn't do it and now you're framing me for your own perverted pleasure?" He put his head in his hands again and rubbed his face. "I really don't need this."

Ronnie was speechless, not to mention out of his depth. The man was either a raving lunatic, or the most confident person on the planet. One minute he was all questions, and the next he was dying of shame. What was with him? Ronnie had not envisaged such opposition. His plan was falling apart.

Giles suddenly turned on him. "If you're so sure it was me, why haven't you gone to the police?"

Bollocks, he hadn't expected that one. "Well…"

"Well what?"

"I thought I'd give you a chance to explain."

"There's nothing *to* explain. I keep telling you I wasn't there…"

The conversation and the protests suddenly stopped. Something had suddenly dawned on Giles. "Oh my God, it's you, isn't it?"

"What's me?" Ronnie asked.

Adi Giles suddenly reached into his little leather bag and pulled out a newspaper. When he'd found the page he wanted, he showed it to Ronnie.

"This." He held up the paper. "You're the man the police are looking for. You're the flasher."

Ronnie's world suddenly fell through his arse, along with half his dinner. His stomach tightened, his throat closed and he suffered palpitations.

He hadn't expected to have the tables turned on him. He suddenly knew he had hit rock bottom. He *knew* he couldn't really prove it. He hadn't seen the man's face. Ronnie never had a phone with him, or a camera. All he'd found was a card. He'd been putting two and two together and making five hundred, never mind five. All he was trying to do was con Giles out of a shortfall to his benefits.

Ronnie put his head in his hands. "Oh, fuck."

It had only taken an instant, but in the moment of time, he suddenly realised his whole life was one big sorry mess. He had nothing and no one, and he'd been living a lie for as long as he could remember. Only now, it had all fallen apart.

He sniffed and snorted and cleared his throat and stared at the man in front of him, one who had probably done no wrong in his life, apart from possibly be in the wrong place at the wrong time, and Ronnie was trying to use it against him. What's more, he *didn't* have any real proof and he knew it. What kind of a shit did that make him? What the hell was he going to do now?

After what seemed an eternity, Ronnie spoke. "Do you know how shit my life is?"

"You think yours is bad, try walking a mile in my shoes," said Giles.

Ronnie suddenly broke down and unloaded the whole shooting match on Giles: how he had been abused by his father as a youngster; the fact that he and his sister had been taken into care when his mother had died and his father had cleared off. And he hadn't seen either his father or his sister for years. How he was existing on benefits. It was a complete pile of shite.

After the barrage, neither man said anything for about five minutes, until Giles broke the ice.

"Look, I'm really sorry for what's happened to you. Really I am, but trying to con me won't help you. It's only a short-term fix. Even if I give you money, you'll only come back for more. And eventually, I will have no more to give. What then? We'll both be done. I'll be broke and there'll be nothing else you can do to me. And when there's nothing else for me to give, what then?"

Ronnie remained silent.

"Well, I'm not going to let that happen," said Giles, wringing his hands together. "Too much of *my* life has been rubbish and I've started to do something about it." He stared hard at Ronnie. "You need help, and I'm going to help you."

Ronnie glanced up, cleared his throat again. "What are you going to do?"

"Look," said Giles, "I know I shouldn't be saying this, but God knows you need it. I think I can help you. Why don't you let me try?"

# Chapter Twenty

Adi Giles left Rodley with his head completely mashed, trying to make sense of the things he'd seen and heard.

Before the meeting in the car park of The Railway Inn he'd had absolutely no idea of the danger he could possibly have been exposing himself to. But whatever had gone through his mind, he had not expected to come face-to-face with, of all people, the Farnley Flasher.

He had no idea what to make of Ronnie Robinson. The man was very obviously unhinged. His appearance and the way he handled himself did not fill Adi with confidence. He'd had something on his mind. Having started off with plenty of bottle, it had soon become obvious to Adi that the man was out of his depth. He was not used to such situations.

Adi wasn't sure what had shocked him more: Ronnie's outrageous accusations, or the fact that he was actually the Farnley Flasher. Whatever possessed him to do such things?

Well, the answer to that was probably quite easy. If Ronnie's claims were true, his treatment and abuse at the hands of his father and a life in care would have been enough to unbalance anyone. It would appear that the area he lived in now was very unsavoury, he had little or no money, and his benefits were apparently being stopped because of a cheating claim. What exactly did the man have to look forward to, apart from a touch of blackmail?

But he was barking up the wrong tree. He'd found a card and put two and two together and made five. He hadn't followed things through properly. He had some wild idea in his head that Adi had killed Max and had then taken photos. What for? That sounded like a gangland execution; *here, kill the man and then prove it to us*. That was way out of Adi's league.

Adi pulled the camper van onto the A6120 Leeds ring road and headed for home, which would probably take him ten minutes.

Back to Ronnie's and his little wild idea; that did bother Adi somewhat. He could easily have dropped a card anywhere within the grounds. But there was a time problem here. Adi was there on Wednesday morning. Ronnie was at the abbey on Tuesday night. Throughout the conversation he was trying to think when he had last visited the abbey. It had to have been two, or maybe three months ago. You wouldn't think a card would survive that long outside, depending on where it had been, of course.

That created another problem. If Ronnie simply had come across a card, why had he suddenly decided to try and blackmail Adi? Why did he think it was Adi Giles in the abbey at midnight on Tuesday night photographing a corpse?

Adi's head was a shed. It was all a complete mess. Situations like these had a very bad habit of escalating. Ronnie might have gone away from the meeting with a glimmer of hope about things, but it didn't mean he wouldn't suddenly change his mind. One drink too many and the whole shooting match could be back on.

But Adi did have an ace up his sleeve. He now had the identity of the flasher, the man the police were searching for, both in connection with what had happened at the abbey, and any other indecent exposure incidents.

The mess his head was in nearly caused him to crash the camper van into a telegraph pole. The sharp blast of a horn from behind made him jump.

"Okay, okay," he shouted. "I didn't hit the bloody thing, did I?"

He glanced at the clock on the dash. Five more minutes and he'd be home. His mind went into a tailspin again.

What if the police did find out the identity of the flasher, and he crumbled, and told them whom he thought the killer was? What if he tried to bargain with them, turn Queen's evidence and tell them they were in it together; but all he'd done was expose himself, in order to get a lighter sentence?

"Don't be stupid. He hasn't got any bloody evidence." He swerved the van back to his side, having drifted into the middle of the road. "Oh Christ, I'm talking to myself now."

And anyway, what the hell was he thinking. Of course there was no evidence, because he wasn't even there in the first place. The police would see right through that one. And as soon as he arrived home, he would disprove Ronnie's ridiculous theory by checking the film in his camera. He'd develop whatever was on there and prove beyond any doubt he'd been nowhere near the place on the night in question.

Adi finally entered the town of Horsforth and pulled off West End Lane, onto Layton Rise. He drove the camper van into the drive and killed the engine. He rested his head in his hands with his elbows on the steering wheel and breathed a deep sigh of relief that he'd actually made it home.

He glanced up, and out of the windscreen. "Oh, my, God, what have I done. I said I would try to help him."

What if he was beyond help? Maybe I can't help someone like Ronnie. Then what? Would the man feel let down once again and decide to create more trouble?

Adi jumped out of the camper, his stomach in knots. He felt sick. How could he have landed in so much trouble?

Letting himself in through the front door he was mildly surprised to hear a radio playing in the kitchen. He walked through and saw Freddie sitting at the table with a coffee.

"Freddie, love, what are you doing home?"

"I have a later start."

Freddie jumped up and immediately poured Adi a coffee. He was dressed and ready for the hotel in grey pleated trousers and a white shirt. His grey tie was on the table, and the jacket on the back of the chair. The hotel might have been a shithole but Freddie had standards, which was one of the things Adi admired. He was almost six feet tall, dark skinned and very slim, with a smooth complexion sporting a George Michael designer stubble.

Freddie put the coffee on the table, planted a kiss on Adi's forehead and sat opposite. "Where you been?" he asked.

Adi didn't know where to start, so he opted with his morning's visit to the solicitor.

"What he say?" asked Freddie, who was Polish, and hadn't yet fully grasped the English language, which Adi found rather cute.

"He thinks I have a chance of maybe getting something out of them."

"The brothers Scrum, you mean?"

"Scum."

"Pardon?"

"The word is scum," said Adi, "not scrum."

Freddie laughed, a hearty chortle. "I never learn your language, no?"

"Nearly," laughed Adi. "Anyway, he's served them with a writ and he's hoping they might cough up. Or at the very least, admit they were wrong to steal my idea."

"Fat chance," replied Freddie. "Pair of snakes. Nasty little creeps. We have word for shit like that in my country: *pasozyt!*"

"That doesn't sound very nice," said Adi. "Anyway, let's not talk about those two, we don't have much time."

"But they rip you off. They cheat you. They deserve to have been taught lesson."

126

"Maybe," said Adi, "but hanging might have been a step too far."

"Not far enough. People like that only learn hard way. Anyway, where else you go?"

Adi couldn't lie to him. He had never lied to anyone. It was not how he lived his life, and if he did, Freddie would see through it.

"Don't get angry, will you?"

"Why I get angry, you not tell me anything yet?"

Adi took a sip of the coffee and then told Freddie about the meeting with Ronnie. He told him everything.

"What?" shouted Freddie.

"You said you wouldn't get angry."

"I didn't. Why always scrum take advantage of you. I hope you take this man to police. It's what he also deserve." Freddie threw his arms in the air. "Jesus Christ, what is wrong with people in this country?"

"Freddie, love, he's troubled. He needs help, not persecuting."

"Maybe, but why have you to help him? What if he makes tables turn on you? What if he get help but still tell police it was you?"

"He wouldn't."

"How you know? Look what he do so far."

Adi dropped his head in his hands. Maybe Freddie was right. All he saw was the good in people. Even if they hurt him he would forgive them and go back for more.

Freddie stood up and put his tie on, patiently threading a Windsor knot; something Adi could simply not do, no matter how much he tried.

"We should think about our future. Please think about what I ask, come back to Poland, let's start life out there. Much better than here. You would be nearer my family, and your parents not far away in Gibraltar."

Adi figured Freddie was probably right. They had no ties here. He rented the posh house from his parents, so they could easily re-rent it to someone else.

"But what about money, Freddie, love. What would we live on?"

"You can take photograph anywhere. I can work hotels anywhere in world and not shithole in Leeds."

"But we'd still need money to get there."

"Not as much as you think. And my family help. And I have money aside."

"Do you have enough?"

Freddie tapped the side of his nose and winked. "I have little sideline at hotel. Gangster men rent rooms and pay me to turn blind eye."

Adi reached out to Freddie. "Oh, God, Freddie, you're not mixed up with them lot, are you?"

"No choice. They come and use hotel anyway. If I agree and make life easy, they pay me and leave me alone. So, yes, we do have enough. We should get away from here. Start new life in Poland."

Adi's mind quickly switched to his afternoon meeting; what if Ronnie turned on him?

"Oh, God, the police have already been once. They think I killed Max because of the court case, and the fact that I never told them about it. All he has to do is tell them it was *me* at the abbey and I'm finished. I'll go to jail for something I didn't do."

Adi was on fire now. "You know what they do to people like us in prison. I won't last two minutes."

Freddie sat down and grabbed Adi's hand. "Calm down. You were not there. You did not kill Max. They cannot put you in prison for something you didn't do."

"Yes, but..."

"Look, I have to go to work but something must I tell you before I go."

"What?" Adi worried about that now. "What are you going to tell me? You don't want us to split up, do you? There's nothing wrong with you, is there? You're not ill. Oh, God, I couldn't handle that. I can face anything if I have you in my life."

"Adi, please, calm down; it not any of those things. Something more bad."

"What? What is it?"

"Have you seen news today?"

"The news. No, why?"

Freddie found his phone, tapped the screen a few times and finally found what he wanted.

"Other scrum brother killed today. Him also hang."

The blood drained from Adi's head. He actually felt it. "No, please tell me that's not true."

Freddie showed him the phone.

"Oh, my, God. I'm done for. That's it. They're coming for me, aren't they?"

"Why you worry?"

"Because Cyril is dead, along with Max. They think I did Max, so they'll certainly think I did Cyril."

"Where were you last night?"

"I was..." Adi stopped dead. "Of course, I was at the theatre."

"Exactly. Alibi. Hundreds more people see you. What you do after show?"

"I went backstage to speak to Mantra."

"More alibi. Whoever is doing this, it is not you." Freddie stood up, kissed Adi's forehead again. "I have work. Tonight you should relax, and don't worry. We speak again tomorrow."

Easier said than done, thought Adi.

After Freddie had left, Adi needed to pull himself together and the best way he could do that was to immerse himself into some photography.

He suddenly remembered what he was going to do when he arrived home. Adi quickly ran upstairs and changed. When he came back down he found his cameras and slipped into his darkroom.

He opened the cameras, removed the film and set about developing whatever was on them. He had taken two or three photos in the morning at the abbey but he couldn't remember what else was on the film, because it had been in the camera a while.

After setting out his stall he took the photographic paper through the three stages needed to produce the results: developer, stop bath and fixer, mixed with water. Whilst he waited for it to take effect he stepped out of the room for another drink.

Thirty minutes later he returned, retrieved the prints from the trays and pegged them on a line. There were more than he'd thought.

Eventually he switched on the light to gain a better view.

Adi suddenly held his breath. They were not what he was expecting; they were, in fact, far from what he was expecting.

# Chapter Twenty-one

The morning after Cyril's departure saw Gardener and Reilly heading up an incident room meeting with the SIO eager to learn what his team had uncovered. Two deaths with a number of suspects that appeared to have alibis, was not helping his confidence. Someone had to be responsible and whoever that was, they were a step ahead of him and his team.

The officers had filed in with folders and tablets and anything else they needed to surrender the information. Once everyone was settled, Gardener checked the whiteboards and started with a question about the identity of the flasher.

"Nothing yet, sir," said Colin Sharp.

"Funnily enough," said Rawson, "plenty of people have come forward to say they've been flashed at in the last few months, but still no one knows who it is."

"Where have they been flashed at?"

"Mostly Farnley, and areas close to there, but the abbey was a first," said Sharp.

Disappointed, Gardener said, "Okay. Keep trying. Put another ad in the paper, see if we can flush him out. If he *has* seen something, we need to know."

"He could be a suspect," said Longstaff.

"It's always possible, Julie," replied Gardener, "but I can't see it. He was there for one reason and one reason only. I doubt he would have killed Max Knowles and then set up some kind of flashing light system, and then ditched his clothes for a flashing of his privates session."

"He'd be drawing too much attention to himself," said Rawson.

"Okay, let's move on. Just to recap, we have Max Knowles found hanged at Kirkstall Abbey, and a few days later, before we can successfully apprehend his murderer, his brother is killed in the same manner but in a different place. What have we found out from the businesses in the area?"

The shop-to-shop results, and a full day in the City Market yielded very little. Very few of the traders actually knew him, or of him. They moved in different circles. Most of them were obviously not working at the suspected time of death. Some of them knew Vera because she often popped in once a week for joints of meat, and fresh vegetables.

"What about the businesses in the same building?" asked Gardener. "Did they have anything to do with him?"

"The accountant and the solicitor," said Bob Anderson. "I suppose it would make sense that he kept stuff in-house, so to speak."

"The accountant looked after the books," said Thornton, "but he seems as tight as they were. He reckoned bills were only paid when they were threatened with being cut off, or legal action, all of which he said was not an offence."

"Maybe not," said Reilly, "but somewhere in amongst that lot we could find someone peeved enough to take revenge."

Gardener nodded. "What about the solicitor, how was he involved?"

"The obvious," said Anderson. "He's representing them in the court case involving Adi Giles. The brothers Knowles were served paperwork yesterday by Giles' solicitor. The matter *is* – or possibly was – going to court."

"Did Cyril know about this?"

"Very likely, it was served the day before he was killed."

There was very little Gardener could question on the matter. He knew about the four files laid out on Cyril's desk because Vera had told them. But he and Reilly had only found three. He mentioned that to the team.

"So who took the missing file?" asked Paul Benson.

"No idea," said Gardener. "We're not sure if the killer took it, which suggests a possible connection to Giles, or that Cyril put it somewhere else. If he did, we have yet to find it."

Gardener turned to Gates and Longstaff. "What about the CCTV on Kirkgate, surely that's revealed something."

"Believe it or not," said Gates, "it hasn't."

"We watched it from four o'clock onwards," said Longstaff, "right up to the point of Cyril leaving via the window. Vera Purdy left at four o'clock like she said she had, and over a period of time, the rest of the people using the building also left."

"The last one being the designer," said Gates. "She left at seven. By that time, Cyril's office light was on. However, there is something worth watching."

Gates set up the laptop connected to the projector, which showed footage of the publisher's demise around eleven o'clock. Following Cyril's exit, which was literally through the window, two figures were seen moving around the room, but they were at the back and it was not clear enough for identification.

"Can we zoom in on that?" asked Gardener.

"We can," said Longstaff, "but it doesn't help, the picture becomes grainy and you have no chance of seeing who it is."

"And to be honest," added Gates, "whoever they are, they are only in that one shot. You can see that they actually cross the room."

"It looks like they're leaving," said Sharp.

"And no one came out of the front door after that?" asked Gardener.

"No," said Gates.

"That means we now *know* two people are responsible," said Reilly, "so there must be a back door to the place."

"Which once again shows that our two people have either done their homework, or they know these two well," said Gardener. "I'd like someone on that, please. Find out if there is a back door, where it is, and is there any CCTV whatsoever that we can pull to help us. If there is, we might hopefully be able to see if one of them is female."

"Do you still think Vera Purdy is responsible?" asked Reilly.

"We can't rule her out, Sean," replied Gardener, "however unlikely it seems. We thought previously that she wasn't up to the physical side of things, unless she had an accomplice. Well, now we can *see* that there are two of them."

"And it's no secret that she feels she can do a better job," said Thornton.

"It's still a long shot," said Gardener, "but not impossible."

"Only problem with that one, boss," said Reilly. "She has an alibi for last night."

Gardener nodded. "Can someone speak to Vera Purdy again and just get the name and number of the taxi company? See when and where they were picked up and dropped off, does it coincide with her version of events?"

Gardener added the notes to the whiteboard, particularly the follow-ups, before moving on to Cyril's home address. The house-to-house in Armley however was pretty much the same story as the business addresses in Kirkstall. It brought very little to the table. No one had anything positive to say about Cyril – most reckon he should have been living a few doors down in the prison.

"That suggests he was a bit of a rogue," said Gardener. "Did anyone elaborate on that one? Had he been up to anything that would have caused someone to kill him?"

"To be honest, sir," said Paul Benson, "it was mostly idle talk and opinions. No one had anything concrete, it was more a case of they didn't trust him because they'd been listening to rumours."

"Did he have any kind of routine?" asked Gardener. "We know Max did."

"Nothing out of the ordinary that we could establish," said Edwards. "He usually left early in the morning and came back at night. He never really went out after he got back home. No one ever actually saw him going shopping but when he came home at night he was usually carrying beers with him."

"It sounds like most of his shopping was done during the day," said Reilly. "He usually ordered Vera Purdy out to get him anything he needed."

"Talking of Vera Purdy, she made a very interesting comment about Adi Giles that we need to follow up," said Gardener. "Have any of you heard of a stage magician, or hypnotist called Mantra?"

"Actually, I have," said Gates. "I've never seen him but my aunt Louise usually goes to his shows. She reckons he's very good."

"I've heard that as well," said Longstaff, "but I'm not really into all that stuff so I don't bother going. I don't mind the illusions, but I'm not into hypnotism."

"Why do you ask?" asked Sharp.

"Vera Purdy reckons that this Mantra treats people privately," said Reilly.

"For what?" asked Rawson.

"No idea," said Reilly, "but she told us her sister pays regular visits, and the last time Vera Purdy was there, to pick her sister up, Giles was sitting in the waiting room."

"That is interesting," said Thornton.

"That's what we thought," replied Gardener, "so we're going to call on him today and see what we can learn."

"She also said that she was at the show last night at the City Varieties, and so was Adi Giles," added Reilly.

"Which possibly rules out Giles killing Cyril," said Anderson.

"Looks like it," said Gardener. "He couldn't possibly be in two places at once. We also spoke to him about the night Max was killed and he claims he was at home."

"Alone," added Reilly.

"So we popped next door and spoke to his neighbours, Steven and Betty Pollard. They couldn't really say. They were out for most of the night. When they left, his van was on the drive. When they returned, it wasn't and the place was in darkness."

"But that was no guarantee," said Reilly. "Sometimes he put the van in the garage and sometimes he didn't."

"We spoke to the others in the small street and it was pretty much the same story," said Gardener. "Most can remember seeing the van in the early evening but not later on. But no one is really interested enough in their neighbours to keep an eye on them. It's that type of area: affluent, with only an interest in themselves. So for now, his alibi stands."

"What's your gut feeling, sir?" Rawson asked Gardener.

"It's one of those things, isn't it, Dave?" said Gardener. "You're damned if you do, and damned if you don't. If I pull him in, I really can't prove anything with what we have so far. If I don't pull him in and something else happens it'll be my fault. But for what it's worth, I think it's highly unlikely that he's behind it."

"No," agreed Reilly. "He's a lover, not a fighter."

Gardener made more notes before turning to the team. "Do we have any further developments with Max's murder? Is there anything we can cross-reference to Cyril's?"

# Chapter Twenty-two

"I've made some headway with the gloves," said Rawson.

"Go on," said Gardener.

"There are a couple of companies. One of them is abroad and the other in London. A firm called Printstar. They specialise mostly in anything you can put a photo on, like cups and mugs and cards and all that sort of stuff. For birthdays and special occasions.

"Anyway, about a year ago somebody came up with a new line in gloves, surgical type of glove, latex, with famous fingerprints."

"And is Lewis Carroll amongst them?" asked Reilly.

"Apparently," said Sharp. "When they first came out they were mostly really famous people. They had Elvis and Frank Sinatra."

"Then some bright spark came up with all sorts of people, including famous murderers. All your top blokes are with them; Yorkshire Ripper, and some of the American killers."

"Okay," said Gardener. "Do we have any records yet?"

"No, but they're onto it," said Rawson. "They're searching through the computer for everyone who has purchased gloves, not just Carroll's but every pair of gloves purchased and sent to this area. We should have something soon."

"Okay," said Gardener, "at least it's positive."

On the subject of the rope there had been no developments. As the team agreed, it could have been bought anywhere and at any time. It could have been stolen from a garage or a site, or someone's shed. It really was a needle in a haystack, as was the print from the Adidas trainers. Nothing had yet come to light.

Rawson admitted there was nothing further on the mask itself. Having spoken to the management team involved with the wrestler who wore them they said the masks had been out of circulation for a number of years. They had originally sold them from their site but not for a long time.

There had been no further developments from the park. The fingertip search had been completed and the team was busy trying to identify anything they had found but, so far, nothing concrete had been handed over.

Gardener glanced at Gates and Longstaff. "What about Max's contacts? Is there a cross-reference with any of Cyril's contacts – in other words, did they have separate clients or was it one big pot?"

"It was a bit of both," said Gates. "They did have separate clients, but then they also had people they both dealt with together. Once again, we're busy working our way through it and trying to contact as many people as possible. We've not come up with anything yet."

"Vera Purdy mentioned spats with other authors," said Gardener. "Did that reveal anything?"

"There were three in particular," said Longstaff. "It would appear that no one was annoyed enough to kill. It was all minor stuff, really. There was a rugby player called Bill Gateford. He was chasing royalties all the time."

"There was a golfer as well," said Gates. "I'm quite surprised, didn't think there were any famous Yorkshire golfers."

"He probably isn't," said Reilly, "if he's going to them two to publish his book."

"Well that one hadn't got off the ground," said Gates. "Apparently it was contractual problems. The golfer, whose name was Dale Martin, if you can believe that, had sent his contract to the Society of Authors to check it, and he was unhappy with some of the stuff. He wanted changes before he would sign it."

"And no doubt Cyril told him where to get off," added Reilly.

"More or less," said Longstaff. "And the other one was involved in cricket, Geoff Holland, but once again, it was a royalty payment problem."

"Had any of these people actually been paid?" Gardener asked.

"No," said Gates, "but judging by the amount they were chasing, none of it was worth killing for."

"And we're happy with their explanations?"

"I think so," said Gates. "Like I said, it was small fry. They probably would have been paid at some time but most of these people have forgotten about it and moved on."

"Okay," said Gardener, "keep cross-checking the names between the two brothers, we might find something."

He moved on to Patrick Edwards. "CCTV and ANPR on the vans in question, Patrick, have we found anything?"

"Yes, and no, sir. All white vans now ruled out. Still working on the rest but I've covered most of them." He consulted a list. "I have about ten more to go through."

"Okay, keep at it. See if you can cover it as soon as possible."

Slightly frustrated at the lack of evidence, Gardener asked if there was anything further to discuss.

Bob Anderson raised his hand. "We've got something interesting to bring to the table."

"Okay, Bob, let's have it, we're in need of something positive."

"After the last meeting," said Thornton, "we decided to pop along to The Ruffin Hotel and check out Adi's boyfriend, Freddie."

"Well done," said Gardener. "Does he exist?"

"Oh definitely," said Anderson. "His name is Fryderyk Kaminska and he originates from Gdańsk, on the Baltic Coast of Northern Poland."

"How long has he been here?"

"He's thirty-five," said Thornton, "left Poland ten years ago. He actually trained as a baker in one of their finest hotels."

"So why did he leave?"

"Unhappy. Apparently they had promised him promotion, prospects, that he'd be given more money, but because of the financial crisis, all of that went by the wayside and he was lucky to have a job at all, so he thought Britain would be a better option."

"How has he ended up in Ruffin Street as a porter?" asked Reilly. "That's hardly a step forward."

"Well," said Anderson, "he was promised pretty much the same thing here. They said they had a position as a chef, but when he got there the bloke they had decided not to leave, and the only thing they had was the night porter's job. Initially he didn't want it but he couldn't find anything else so he went back."

"But he hates it," said Thornton. "Doesn't like working nights, doesn't like the job and doesn't want to be here any longer."

"But that's not the only thing he hates," said Anderson.

"No," said Thornton, "he hates the brothers scum as he calls them, the Knowles."

"For what they've done to *him*, or his boyfriend?" asked Reilly.

"For what they've done to his boyfriend," said Anderson. "He believes they have ripped Adi off royally, and that they deserve everything they get. He was only surprised that someone hadn't done it sooner."

"He didn't hold back, then?"

"No."

"So what's your gut instinct, Bob?" asked Gardener. "Does he hate them enough to kill?"

"I don't know, boss," replied Anderson, "but I think we need to spend more time on him. We have the name of the hotel in Gdańsk."

That changed the atmosphere in the room. Gardener turned to the whiteboards and made his updates.

"In that case, speak to them and speak to Interpol and see if he has any form for anything."

"Will do," said Anderson.

"Okay," said Gardener, "let's revisit our suspects list. We wondered about Cyril being responsible but I think *his* death has ruled him out. Vera Purdy and Adi Giles have alibis, but they might still be in the frame. I believe we can now add three more names to those, looking at the files we found on Cyril's desk.

"I'd like someone investigating Hunslet Printers. It's not likely the company are involved, but there may be an individual who isn't happy and wants to take matters into their own hands.

"Duncan Preston, the ex-Leeds footballer. He was taking them to court, but was he fed up of waiting?"

"And the infamous, Danny Drake, landlord and general scumbag," said Reilly. "He's pretty much into every racket going but I'm not sure he's a killer."

"Probably not, Sean," said Gardener. "Chances are he would have evicted them if he'd been fed up enough."

Gardener then addressed the rest of the team. "Which leaves us with someone new, a fourth name; Polish Freddie. He has the motive, and he may have the time. If he works in Ruffin Street and the place is as bad as we know it to be, we have to question, is he actually there all night, and if he isn't, does anyone care enough to check?" He nodded to Anderson and Thornton. "I'd like you two on his case."

# Chapter Twenty-three

When the front door opened, the last thing Gardener expected to see was a man standing there in a mask. He would find it quite unnerving under normal circumstances, but when the mask being worn was an exact replica of one directly connected to his investigation, it was even more unsettling.

Even Reilly held his tongue.

They held up warrant cards and Gardener introduced them as part of the West Yorkshire Major Incident Team.

"My, my, that was quick."

Unsure of what else to say, Gardener opened his batting with: "Mr Mantra?"

"At your service." He held the door open wider. "Please, come through and let me pour you gentlemen a drink."

Without waiting for any further discussion, he turned and walked down a long hall with a twisting staircase leading up to the next level, thick carpets and expensive oils, through to a stainless-steel kitchen the entire width of the house. In the middle was an island housing hobs and cooker tops, with every utensil mentionable hanging down from hooks. The patio doors led out on to one of the longest and largest gardens Gardener had ever seen. The room was warm and he could smell fresh coffee. In one corner of the room a radio played something classical.

"Please, take a seat," said Mantra, pointing to a larger than usual breakfast bar, which was in fact one of two.

When both men sat, he brought over the drinks with sugar and milk on a tray, and a plate full of biscuits, which would have won over Reilly immediately.

"We can't keep calling you Mantra," said Gardener. "Do you have a name?"

He nodded, taking a seat himself. "Thornley, Brian Thornley."

He was tall, and dressed all in black: trousers, shirt, shoes – even the mask. From what Gardener could see the man's teeth were perfect but he had the blackest, deepest eyes. Gardener couldn't begin to describe the voice, other than as something blocking a waste disposal. There had to be a story, though Gardener didn't think they would hear about it today.

"I must say the service from you people is first class. I only called about fifteen minutes ago."

"Called?" questioned Reilly.

"Yes. In fact I only really found out about thirty minutes ago but I had to make sure before reporting it."

"Reporting what?" asked Reilly.

The eyes behind the mask narrowed. Gardener realised there was a problem, and the man probably thought they were here for another reason.

"A theft, officer. I've been burgled. I realise it isn't much but it is worth reporting anyway."

"We're from the Major Incident Team, Mr Thornley," said Gardener. "We're not calling in connection with your theft."

"Oh, I'm so sorry, please forgive me. I've put two and two together, saw you standing outside..."

"Not to worry," said Gardener, "but just for the record, what has gone missing?"

Mantra smiled. "It's nothing really, just some old ropes from what I can see."

Gardener's spine tingled for a second time in as many minutes. "When did you notice they had gone?"

"As I said, about half an hour ago. But it could have been any time in the last month or so. You see, I rarely venture down to the shed. I leave all that to my gardener."

"And he hasn't noticed?"

"Can't have done," said Mantra, "but they're probably not as important to him."

"Why did you go down to the shed today?" asked Reilly.

"I was looking for some WD40, a problem with a faulty lock."

"Can you give us a description of the ropes?" asked Reilly, drinking the coffee and leaving a large hole in the plate of biscuits.

"Hardly," replied Mantra. "I imagine all ropes look the same. But it's no bother, I can buy some more. I just thought if anything more came of it, a crime number might come in handy."

"We'll be sure to mention it back at the station," said Reilly. "Do you use ropes in your act?"

"I have been known to."

"Are you a magician or an illusionist?" asked Gardener. "Apart from being a hypnotist?"

Mantra laughed. "I suppose they are one and the same. We all make things disappear and reappear, and fool people into thinking that's what we've actually done."

"So," said Reilly, "are you a member of that Magic Circle?"

"I used to be."

"What exactly is that?"

"It's a British organisation, pretty much dedicated to promoting and advancing the art of magic."

143

"And how do you actually get in?"

"Applicants have to qualify for membership, either through a performance exam or by a written thesis on a branch of magic, after which they will be a designated member of the Magic Circle."

Before they asked another question, Mantra continued. "It was founded by a group of magicians in 1905 as a private magicians' club."

"You said, used to be," pointed out Gardener. "Are you no longer a member?"

"No, not these days, but I can still perform in the theatres because I'm a fully paid-up member of equity."

Reilly made a note.

"Why do you use ropes?" asked Gardener.

"Mainly for hanging illusions."

There it was again, thought Gardener.

"You actually hang someone on stage?" asked Reilly.

"Not for real."

"So what *do* you do?"

Mantra took them through *The Phantom of the Opera* scene that he had recently performed at the City Varieties, which struck a chord with Gardener when he thought back to someone else they'd investigated who'd hung an aged thespian on the stage of the Grand Theatre in Leeds in front of his audience.

"How does that work?" asked Reilly. "How do you hang someone but you don't, and then make it look like you have?"

"Mr Reilly," said Mantra, "are you asking me to give away my trade secrets?" He laughed again but then continued to tell them. "The normal method for hanging scenes is a breakaway noose, where the noose is fake and actually lies quite loose around the actor's neck. Meanwhile, the actor is suspended from a harness.

"The audience should see nothing: not the hook at the back of the noose, not the choreography. Everything should be believable. Ideally the audience isn't going to be

144

aware of any of it. If they ever feel like it's unsafe, then it's wrong. The audience wants to totally believe in the story."

Mantra stood up and poured himself a fresh coffee, offering Gardener and Reilly one. Gardener declined but Reilly was happy to appease, if only so he could mop up the remainder of the biscuits.

"What about the rabbit out of the hat trick?"

"That's an old one," replied Mantra, sitting down. "There are three ways to sell it. The most obvious is to use a table with a hidden drawer big enough to fit a rabbit. Add a concealed hole for the magician to reach through and you can get a rabbit in a hat. The second is to install a secret compartment inside the hat, slide the compartment door open to reveal a rabbit inside.

"The final way is when a magician uses sleight of hand, with a rabbit sitting in a bag hooked to a table. While waving their arms around, the rabbit is whisked out of the bag and produced from the back of the magician's hand into the hat."

Before another question was asked, Mantra asked one of his own. "Now you gentlemen said Major Incident Team and you've admitted you're not investigating the theft, so it must be something a little more serious. How can I help you?"

"We'd like to talk to you about hypnotism," said Gardener, "particularly the private treatment you offer to some people."

"Okay."

"Do you know a man called Adrian Giles?"

"I do, yes."

"Can you tell me in what capacity?"

"May I ask why?"

"Let's just say he has come up in our investigation and *we* would like to know a little more about him. We do have it on good authority that you offer private counselling sessions."

"With all due respect, officers, that really would come under client confidentiality."

"Okay, Mr Thornley," said Gardener, "this *is* a murder investigation. We could, if you want us to, obtain a warrant."

"A murder investigation?"

"Yes."

"In that case, there is no need to obtain a warrant. I'll help you as much as I can. I suspect that this interview is confidential, and I would hope you respect my willingness to help and that you will keep all information to yourselves."

"Of course," said Gardener. He noticed Reilly had his pad and pen at the ready.

"Is he suspected of murdering someone?"

"His name has come up in the investigation more than once."

Mantra smiled and nodded. "I would imagine this has something to do with the gentleman who was found hanged at Kirkstall Abbey. And before you ask, I do read the papers, I do watch the news, and Adrian Giles came to see me yesterday in a terrible state. He told me he had found the man in question."

"Seems like you're well versed in the matter, Mr Thornley," said Gardener.

"What would you like to know?"

"Why are you treating him; what are you actually treating him for?"

"His biggest problem is anxiety."

"That doesn't surprise me," said Reilly.

"Anxiety is a terrible condition, officer. The best way to describe it is panic attacks. You feel out of control of your life, which can cause mild depression. You worry unduly about silly things, you're constantly ill at ease, worrying, worrying, worrying... if you get the picture."

"That certainly sums your man up," said Reilly. "We spoke to him on the morning of the hanging and he was definitely on edge. We could understand that having just found a corpse at the end of a rope, it would be unnerving, but he seemed a little over the top."

"That's how it can take you. We've all suffered it from time to time, some more than others. Imagine the feeling you get when you are late for something important, the feeling just before an exam, or when a policeman calls... but imagine getting that feeling over everything in life, even the smallest things, and nothing takes that feeling away.

"He came to see me because he was recommended by a friend. We have made some headway, or should I say, had, until he found the man hanging in the abbey. I believe he was there on an assignment. I take it you know he's a photographer. He was there on the morning in question, taking photographs for a new book. When he found the man hanging, it put all our work almost back to square one. But I am certain we can get his confidence back again."

"How long have you been seeing him?" Gardener asked.

"Three months, maybe," replied Mantra. "It started when he discovered he'd been ripped off by a publisher. A book that had been all his doing was eventually published under their name. Which, of course, I'm sure you know, happens to be the publisher who was hanged. So I can certainly see your predicament."

"How did he seem when he came to see you about that?"

"Beside himself. He was totally consumed with grief, worried about everything, and wondering what he should do about it."

"So he wasn't out for revenge?" asked Reilly.

"Not at all," replied Mantra. "He doesn't have it in him. I understand you're investigating a serious crime, officers, but I don't believe for one minute he's your man."

Gardener stood up, realising there was little else he could ask. "Thank you for your time, Mr Thornley. I'm sorry to hear about the burglary but we will make inquiries when we get back."

"Very nice of you, thank you."

As they made for the front door, Gardener turned. "Do you mind if I ask you a personal question?"

"You're wondering about the mask, and why I wear it indoors, at home, and pretty much everywhere I go."

Gardener nodded, wondering if he should add clairvoyant to the long list of Mantra's credits.

"Personal reasons, Mr Gardener. Many years ago, something happened that I found pretty traumatic. I feel that if I cannot see my face, it isn't there; no constant reminder of that day."

Gardener tipped his hat. "My apologies. I was just curious."

Mantra smiled. "No need to apologise. I hope I've been of service to you."

"Yes, thank you."

The front door closed and the pair of them made their way up the path toward the gate and the road, when a man suddenly appeared, dressed in a faded green boiler suit and woolly hat, pushing a wheelbarrow full of garden waste.

"Been to see Lord Tightarse, have we?"

"I'm sorry?" asked Gardener.

"Him in there, what's he been telling you?"

"You are?" asked Reilly.

"Tom Jenkins, gardener, general dogsbody, and unpaid help."

"What do you mean, Mr Jenkins?" asked Gardener.

"All this," – he dropped the barrow handles and spread his arms wide – "it's all for show, you know. He's got no money. Doesn't work half as much as he used to. Not paid me or the window cleaner for three months."

"He must have some money," said Reilly, "otherwise how would he pay for the upkeep of the house?"

"Well if he has he's keeping it close to his chest, that's all I can say."

"You're the gardener, you say?" asked Gardener.

"Aye, and everything else."

"What do you know about the burglary?"

"What burglary?"

"Apparently he's had some stage props stolen from the shed," said Reilly. "He reported it, and he thought that was why we were here."

"I don't know anything about any burglary," said Jenkins, removing his hat and scratching his head. "Anyway, if you're not here about the burglary, what the hell are you here for?"

"Nothing important," said Gardener. "So, are you saying he hasn't had any props stolen?"

"Couldn't tell you, I wouldn't know. He might have done. Like as not he's done it himself and trying to claim some compo."

With that, Tom Jenkins picked up the barrow and continued on his not-so-merry way.

# Chapter Twenty-four

Adi knocked on the door and waited.

With a blue sky, and a clean atmosphere, the day was unusually warm. But he didn't feel safe. Ronnie had parked his car on the front garden but to use the word park was an overstatement. From the position it was in it could only have been airlifted and simply dropped.

Glancing around, the garden resembled something out of the Amazon rain forest. All manner of things grew in all manner of directions, most of which wouldn't have been out of place in *The Day of The Triffids*. The exterior of the house nearly outclassed the garden if grot had been the key word; it couldn't have been painted since new. Lying in front of the car were three roof tiles, and an overflowing dustbin.

A screaming teenager flew by on a bike. The Lord only knows what he had shouted to one of his friends but Adi couldn't see anyone else so he suspected the other teenager was probably in Manchester. Opposite the house was an area of greenery, but it was so overgrown it simply resembled a bigger version of Ronnie's garden.

He was suddenly reminded of the TV program *Keeping Up Appearances*, in which one Hyacinth Bucket did her best to distance herself from her brother-in-law, Onslow, who lived in a place exactly like Ronnie's; the polar opposite of where she lived.

The door opened and Adi caught sight of a man who had obviously made the effort, but had perhaps employed Mary Quant as his style guru. Ronnie was wearing an orange shell suit that Adi hadn't seen the likes of before, with a pair of white Adidas trainers.

Ronnie was an odd character at the best of times but he'd not been given a good start in life when it came to appearances. He was rather skinny, balding, with rodent-like features: small mouth, bucked teeth, small nose and a pair of slit like eyes, all pushed together as if his face had been moulded in a hurry; the result of an accident in the pottery shop. He wasn't all that tall either. To top it all off, Ronnie had odd eyes – one brown, the other green. And Adi thought *he* had problems.

"Well don't stand there all day."

"Why? Am I letting too much fresh air in?"

Ronnie clearly didn't understand the joke. "For God's sake, get in, I don't want the neighbours talking."

"You mean they don't already?" asked Adi, glancing around.

Adi stepped inside and closed the front door, staring at the living room. He may not have felt safe outside but in here he sensed a whole new dimension of fear.

"Park yourself," said Ronnie. "I cleaned up specially for you."

When, thought Adi, 1951? The World Health Organization would have a field day in here. Even Covid-19 would struggle to survive a night. The brown curtains were threadbare, as was the grey cord carpet. Nothing matched. All the furniture was different. The hi-fi had probably been a seventies prototype, and wouldn't surprise Adi if it had valves. He noticed an old Commodore computer on a table near the TV, and a pile of magazines in each corner of the room. The stale smell suggested the windows had never been opened.

"Come on, sit down, kettle's boiled."

Having gained Ronnie's trust it would be impolite not to do as he was being asked.

Ronnie disappeared and returned a few minutes later with two mugs of tea. To give him credit, the mugs must have been brand new. He placed the drinks on a coffee table and stared at Adi.

"So, what's up? You sounded dead worried on the blower."

"Worried would be an understatement," replied Adi. "I just can't believe how my life's turning out."

"I'll swap you any day," said Ronnie.

"You won't after you've seen these." Adi reached into his bag and drew out a Manila file. It was pointless beating about the bush. The matter needed some attention and he had no idea at all on how to proceed.

"After we'd finished the other day," said Adi, "I went home and decided to check my camera. I knew there was some old film in one of them that needed developing."

"Dead clever that," said Ronnie.

"What? Remembering I needed to develop a film?"

"No, for Christ's sake, developing the bloody things."

"Wish I hadn't now."

"Why? Can't be all that bad."

Adi opened the folder and placed the photos on Ronnie's knee. "See if you still think that when you've seen them."

The expression on Ronnie's face darkened. "Why, how bad are they?"

"Just look at them for God's sake."

"Okay, okay. Is there a fucking war on somewhere?"

"Oh, God," said Adi, chewing the nail of one of his fingers. "I don't know what to do."

The photos he was showing Ronnie were mostly from the night at the abbey, when Max Knowles had been hung. There were around a dozen of them: long shots, close ups, detailed stuff. Max's face was clearly shown, as was the rope around his neck, and a close up of the knot around the beam, though God only knew how that one had been captured.

Ronnie's face paled when he saw them. "Oh, Christ."

"Precisely."

"*You've* taken all these of that bloke who was killed?"

"No."

"What do you mean, no? You just said you developed them from your camera. You must have taken them."

"I keep telling you, I wasn't there." At least that was what he believed.

Adi was devastated. Somehow or other, the photos went some way to proving he *had* been at the abbey on the night of Max's death. He had taken photos of Max and other places around the building. *But why? How? Why couldn't he remember? What was going on? Was he finally cracking up? Did he have a serious illness that blanked you out from time to time so you didn't know what you were doing?* Biggest question, had he killed Max? He could not remember doing so. His head was a complete mess.

Ronnie suddenly stood up and walked around the room. Returning to his seat, he trawled through the photos again, as if somehow they might all have disappeared by the time he sat down again.

"You haven't seen them all," said Adi.

Ronnie stared at him. "You mean there's more?"

"Those at the bottom, you haven't finished."

Ronnie quickly grabbed them and checked them out. The last few were much worse, because they showed Cyril, hanging from his office window.

"Oh, Christ," said Ronnie. "This is really bad."

"Tell me about it."

Ronnie glanced up quickly. "Are there any of me?" he asked.

Adi had one inside his bag that he was going to leave out but Ronnie had a right to know. The shot was of the arched abbey window and the view of the grounds beyond. Once you peered closely enough at the photo, the shape of a head in a mask began to materialise, peeking over the ledge at whoever was taking them.

"Oh, Christ."

"What do you mean, oh Christ?" asked Adi. "You knew you were there. You haven't denied it."

"I know I haven't, but it's a bit different when you see yourself." Ronnie continued to stare at the photo before asking, "What are you going to do about it?"

"What do you mean?"

"Will you stop asking me that?" shouted Ronnie, causing Adi to flinch. He hated being shouted at. "What do you think I mean? Now you have all this shit in your possession, what are you going to do about it?"

"I can hardly go to the police, can I?"

"Not unless you have a hell of a story," replied Ronnie.

"Going to them would put me in a terrible position. I'd automatically be seen as the killer. How could I possibly talk my way out of that one?"

Adi Giles jumped straight into the next set of questions before Ronnie had even digested the first round.

"And what should I do about you? What would I tell the police about you? They'd want to know if I know you, and if we're in league together. How bad would that be?"

"What do you mean?"

"Look," shouted Adi, "you've just told me to stop asking you that, now you're at it."

"Sorry, but what did you mean by that comment?" Before giving Adi a chance to speak, Ronnie had a meltdown. "This is just the icing on the fucking cake. I'm sick to death of my life. Everything I had has gone."

Christ, thought Adi, did he even have anything to start with?

Ronnie steamed on. "I'm not getting any money from anywhere. I can't run my car. I can't eat; do you know I'm having to steal my fucking meals? I won't be able to pay my bills. There's nothing left for me. I don't even enjoy flashing. It's wrong. I should never have done it in the first place. Do you know what I feel like doing?"

"Don't say going to the police, please."

"Going to them might be the easiest solution. Getting banged up would solve all my problems. No, what I feel like doing is ending it all, topping myself. Tell me, what have I got left to live for?"

Tears rolled down Ronnie's face. Adi put his hands to his mouth and then one on Ronnie's shoulder.

"Don't say that. There's always something to live for, we just have to find it. We're both in a mess, but we can't give in. We have to find a solution to this. I've agreed to help you. I can't simply betray you."

Although he had only recently met Ronnie, and the chances were he had been going to blackmail Adi, all of that was down to the deep-rooted problems he'd had in his life. He was in a terrible state, and so was Adi, but he had to think what it would do to Ronnie if he reported him to the police as the Farnley Flasher. They'd ask if he had proof, and he would have to show them, then that would be it. Curtains!

After some minutes of silence, Adi suggested there was only one course of action he could take.

"What?" asked Ronnie.

"I need to hide the photos."

"What good will that do?"

"It'll give me time to think," said Adi.

"But what about me?" questioned Ronnie.

"Have you ever tried hypnotherapy?"

"Hypno what?"

"Have you ever been hypnotised?"

"You mean like them silly bastards on the telly that fall asleep and then get up and strut around like a chicken? I don't think so, thank you very much."

"I'm being serious. I have a friend who could help you. He could get to the bottom of your problems and start to help you live a better life."

"That would take years, I don't think either of us will live that fucking long."

"Just give it a try. I'm seeing him, and he's helping me." Although Adi had said that, he wasn't quite sure it was true. "You should let me set something up for you. I'll pay for the first few sessions and see if it helps. Give it a try, please."

"I'm not sure."

"What have you got to lose?"

"Probably nothing," replied Ronnie, "but that's not really our biggest problem, is it? These are." He held up the photos. "You see, there's something I just can't get my head round."

"What?"

"Well, if you didn't take them," said Ronnie, "who did?"

"How do I know? All I know is, it can't have been me."

"Why not?" asked Ronnie. "It's your camera."

"Oh, Jesus," said Adi, placing his head in his hands, wishing the whole world would simply leave him alone. "I don't believe this, but I just *know* it wasn't me."

"Maybe you *do* know that inside, but you can't prove it, can you?" said Ronnie. "What a fucking mess. You'll never prove you weren't there, not with these. I definitely *was* there, and wished I wasn't. Do you sleepwalk?"

"Sleepwalk?" asked Adi, wondering what the hell he was talking about.

"That's what I asked."

"Sleepwalk," he repeated. "Have you any idea how stupid that sounds? You're asking if I got up, put my clothes on, packed my cameras, left the house, drove to Kirkstall, killed somebody, took photos, and then drove back and got back into bed? Sleepwalking is one thing but isn't that pushing things a bit *too* far?"

"Well... when you put it like that."

"How else can you put it? I'm not from outer space, I can't make myself invisible, or teleport myself all over the world. I only wish I could right now."

"Okay, keep your hair on."

"I am keeping my hair on, but come on, that really is stretching things. Do you have any better suggestions?"

"Only one."

"Go on, then, let's hear it."

"Could someone have nicked your camera?"

"Nicked my cam..." Adi suddenly froze when he thought about the implications of that suggestion.

There was only one person in the world he knew who could have done that; only one person who hated Cyril and Max as much as he did. And Adi lived with him.

But why?

# Chapter Twenty-five

Mantra sat back and stared up at the ceiling.

They were in the living room, sitting in chairs with a coffee table between them. Two cups of tea, a sugar bowl, a milk jug, and a plate of Danish pastries – remained untouched. The room was pleasantly warm but Adi Giles felt like a block of ice on the inside.

In a short space of time his world had turned to shit.

Mantra leaned forward and picked up the photos again, staring at each of them in turn. Adi Giles was close to tears. He knew there was enough evidence here to sink a battleship.

"I don't know what to do, I really don't. I don't know what to say. I really thought we were getting somewhere. You were helping me with my anxiety, putting me on the right track. After I'd been to see you I could genuinely feel myself coming down. I was more relaxed than I had ever been.

"I didn't worry about all the stupid things, like was each remote control with the correct machine? Were all the double and triple lights switches in the house facing the same way? Were the toilet rolls in the bathroom the right way round? Have you any idea how stupid all that sounds? Most normal people would laugh at that stuff, but you didn't. You accepted it all and tried to help me. Now I'm finished, back at square one. Worse than that, I might be facing a murder charge."

"It's not my job to laugh at people, Adrian. I'm here to help, especially when someone is paying me money for therapy sessions. What kind of a person would I be if I laughed at you for some of the things you have told me? They may not mean a great deal to most people, but to you they are life and death. And that is why you came to me. You needed help."

Adi Giles took a sip of tea, carefully. The way he was feeling now he could drop the cup at any given moment, and that would be bad. In fact he couldn't think of anything worse, apart from the photos, and what they represented.

"What are we going to do?" he asked. "Do you see any way out of this mess?"

"There's always a way out of a mess," replied Mantra. "It's simply a case of finding the right solution."

Adi put the cup back on the coffee table when he heard what Mantra had said. It was the safest place for it.

"Do you mean that?" he said. "Do you really mean it?"

"Yes. We simply have to approach this logically."

"How?"

"We examine the evidence like the police would, and we try to arrive at a conclusion that will benefit all of us... including them."

"I can't see how," replied Adi, and he couldn't. On a scale of global cataclysmic events, the photos were right up there with the pandemic as far as he was concerned. "I'll do anything. Please, tell me, what do I have to do?"

"Well first of all, let's see what you can remember of the night itself. You say you did not kill Max Knowles. You did not take any photos, in fact, you were not there at all."

"I didn't, I know I didn't."

"But can you prove it?"

"What do you mean?"

"What I say," replied Mantra. "Can you prove you were not there when Max was being killed? Let's be honest, the abbey will have CCTV, so there would be evidence."

Adi Giles stopped to think about it.

"However," said Mantra, "if there *had* been CCTV evidence, the police would have had you already. So that's a plus for you. What can you actually remember about that night? It wasn't that long ago, so what do you actually recall about the night itself?"

Adi sat and thought before speaking. "Well I remember getting all the equipment together."

"Where?"

"It's all in the darkroom. That way I know where it is and I'm not running around the house like a headless chicken trying to find the smallest, most important piece."

Mantra held a hand up. "Please, try to keep calm. Good. What time?"

"It would have been half past seven. I'd just finished watching Emmerdale. I always watch that. Love the characters, and the fact that it's set round here."

"Adrian," said Mantra, "stick with me, please; don't deviate. So, you watched your program, and then you sorted out the equipment you needed. How long did that take?"

"About half an hour."

"So we're now approaching eight o'clock, yes?"

"Yes."

"What next?"

"I think I went for a shower."

"Only think?"

"Yes, I did go for a shower. Then I came down and poured myself a glass of Baileys."

"Did you see your neighbours at any point during the course of the evening?"

Adi couldn't work that question out. "No, I hardly ever see them. Why?"

"Because they would help with an alibi. What did you do next?"

Adi scratched his head and ruffled his hair. "I think I remember the phone ringing. Yes, it did, I'm sure it did."

"Who called you?"

"I don't know."

"You don't know? Why don't you know? Do you have your phone with you?"

"Yes." Adi pulled it out of his pocket and worked his way through the menu, checking for all the calls made and received. His heart suddenly stopped.

"What's wrong?" asked Mantra.

"The call history has been deleted. No, God no, it can't be." Adi's stomach suddenly lurched, threatening a bowel emptying session. He passed the phone over. "Look, I only have yesterday, the rest has gone."

Mantra checked.

"Why would it have been deleted? Did you do that?"

Adi stared at Mantra, deflated. "I wouldn't have thought so. I know I delete every text but I've never found out how to delete the call history."

"But why would you?"

"I can't stand mess and lists, it's all junk. I like to delete everything and keep it clean. And that way no one can catch me out on anything." Adi stood up and scratched himself. He was starting to itch all over. "Why am I like I am, for God's sake?"

"I beg to differ about catching you out," replied Mantra, "sometimes, as in this case, it would be good proof of a fact we need to check. Nevertheless, your provider will be able to give us a transcript if we need it. I do find it odd that you delete every text but you've not discovered how to do it with your calls and yet here it is, empty. It begs the question if not you, then who?" The hypnotist paused before continuing. "Okay, can you remember anything after the phone call?"

Adi shook his head, desperately trying to recollect anything. "No, nothing."

"So what is the next thing you remember?"

"Wait a minute." Adi put his head in his hands and thought hard, but nothing came to him. "Oh, God, this is awful. The only thing I know is, I woke up in the chair.

The TV was still on and it was something ridiculous like two in the morning."

"And you can't remember anything in between?"

"No." Adi felt completely hollow, and drained of energy, as if he'd been run over by a steamroller.

"Okay, Adrian. Maybe you simply fell asleep. Sit back in the chair, let's try some hypnotherapy; see if we can get to the bottom of this."

Mantra reached for a pocket watch.

Thirty minutes later, Adi Giles was woken up and brought back to reality.

"Where am I?"

"Relax, Adrian. You're here with me, Mantra, do you remember me?"

"Yes," – he sat bolt upright – "of course I do. What happened?"

"Sit back, relax, allow yourself time to come round." Mantra passed his guest some tea. "Here, I made it fresh before I woke you up."

Adi took it and sipped it. He remembered what they had done and why. "Did you find anything out?"

Mantra sat down. "I wish I had. I'm so sorry, but whatever happened, you have blanked it from your memory completely. I tried to get to the bottom of it but you became very agitated, and I didn't think it would be wise to continue with you in that state."

Close to tears again, Adi said, "What are we going to do. I can't go to prison, and I will for something like this, a double murder. They'll throw away the key. I can't go, I really can't. I can't do the time. They're filthy, horrible places. Oh, God, we have to do something."

The itching started again, quite quickly.

"It's okay," said Mantra. "Let me ask you the question outright. Did you kill Max Knowles?"

"No," screeched Adi. "I know I didn't."

"Did you kill Cyril?"

"No."

"Yet you have evidence here that proves otherwise. If the police find these photos they will use them against you."

"Not if I hide them, or destroy them."

"Apart from printed versions, do you have digital versions?"

"I'm not sure," said Adi, "I might have; I might have backed everything up on the computer. I usually do."

"Then they will find them, which will make things worse for you, make you look more guilty than you are. No matter how clever you are with computers, they have teams of people who are much brighter, and they have many tricks up their sleeves for recovering data."

"What am I going to do?" Adi started biting his nails.

"Even if you managed to destroy them, you'll never be able to withstand the questioning from the police. Look at you now, and this is not a jail cell, it's a friendly atmosphere."

"What do you think I should do?"

"Perhaps honesty is the best policy."

"You mean tell them about the photos?"

"It might be better to try to clear your name. Otherwise the guilt will eat away at you. But I am not the best person to advise on that one. You must speak with your solicitor and tell him what you've told me, show him these and see what he advises."

Adi put the tea on the table, feeling totally destroyed. "Maybe you're right."

"But let's look at another possible option."

"Go on."

"I believe you when you tell me you didn't kill either of them, and that you didn't take the photos. But if you didn't, who did?"

He'd already been asked that question once today, and he really didn't want to think of the alternative, because he simply couldn't bring himself to believe it.

"I know," said Mantra, "before you even tell me, that you have an answer to that question."

Adi put his head in his hands. He really didn't want to accept the facts. He didn't want it to be Freddie, but it had to be one of them, and he was totally convinced it wasn't him. But why didn't he know for certain? Why couldn't he recall the night? How had he managed to blank it to the point that even the hypnotist couldn't draw it out of him? Had Freddie suddenly come home from work? Sometimes he does. If he had, did he drug Adi's Baileys?

He put his head in his hands again. No, please, no. He didn't want to think that way. But what the hell had happened that night?

"You know I'm right, don't you?" said Mantra. "But you don't want me to be."

Adi stood up. "I need time to think this through."

"Of course you do," said Mantra, "but please don't take too long. The last thing you want is the police knocking at your door and catching you unawares with this lot on you. Please seek legal advice, and put this matter to bed. And if you need to speak to me again, please don't hesitate."

"Thank you," said Adi.

He collected his belongings and placed them back in his little leather bag.

"Now you mention it, there is one thing I would like to ask."

"Of course, what is it?"

"I have a friend in your waiting room."

"Yes, I saw him come in with you."

"Would you please do me a big favour? His name is Ronnie, and I think he's in as big a mess as me."

"What? He thinks he's killed someone as well?"

"No, not that bad. But it took me a lot to persuade him to come along. Would you at least give him half an hour to see if you can help?"

163

Mantra stared at his watch, before saying. "I really shouldn't see anyone without an appointment."

"I understand, but you really would be helping me... and him."

Mantra nodded. "I have a few minutes."

# Chapter Twenty-six

Thirty minutes later, Ronnie was back in the waiting room, and Adi was back in the living room.

"That was quick," said Adi. "What happened? You can't have hypnotised him."

Mantra shook his head. "I'm afraid I can't help your friend."

"Why not? Has he done something wrong? Has he upset you? What's wrong with him?"

Mantra held his hand up again. "Please, calm yourself. It's none of those things. I can't help him because he needs professional help."

"I thought you were a professional," said Adi.

"I am, but he is way beyond my remit. Cast your mind back to when you came to see me for the first time. You were in a terrible state."

"Don't remind me," said Adi.

"Why was that?"

"I was worried."

"And why were you worried?"

"I was worried about everything," said Adi. "Always have been, I've had it all my life."

"Precisely," replied Mantra, "but I didn't know that. So we used the hypnotherapy technique to get to the bottom of your problem, and everything came out. Your homosexuality was causing you great concern, not because you *were* one, but because of the incident at school, and the beatings you received from the other children. Anxiety was eating away at you."

Adi's eyes misted over, as he remembered how cruel children could be. But it wasn't only children; he'd also suffered at the hands of bigoted adults since.

"But I can't use this type of therapy on Mr Robinson."

"Why?"

"Firstly, because he knows why he is like he is. I must point out here that he has allowed me to share his personal information with you. It started with the abuse as a child, then his mother dying, and he and his sister being taken into care, and he was still treated badly. I can't regress him to find all that out. He's aware of it already."

Adi sat back. Nothing was going according to plan. What the hell was he going to do? He doubted he could help himself out of his own mess, and he probably wouldn't be able to help Ronnie with his. But he'd promised he would.

"However, I have given him the names of people who may be able to help. As for me, I simply can't."

# Chapter Twenty-seven

Gardener and Reilly arrived back at the station, parked the car, and made their way up to the incident room.

"Sean, can you sort out a couple of drinks, please? I'll see who's around."

Although the room was a hive of activity, he couldn't actually see any of his team. He knew they wouldn't be far away because it was approaching five o'clock. They had been out in the field all day and the chances of catching people after normal hours were scant at best.

But did they have anything for him?

Reilly returned not only with drinks but he'd somehow managed to find a plate with a few cakes and some biscuits. Gardener didn't ask him where he'd found them but he suspected a number of officers somewhere would have a fair idea who had them.

"Look who I found?"

"What do you mean?" said Gardener, eyeing the food.

Reilly stepped to one side and Benson and Edwards appeared.

"Grab a seat and tell me all you know," said Gardener.

"Not much," offered Benson, reaching out for a cake.

Reilly retracted the plate. "Come on, son, you know the rules. You have to earn the cake."

"Are you serious?" questioned Benson. "You probably nicked them anyway."

"Until you can prove that, son, these remain my property."

Edwards found the incident hilarious as Benson gave in and parted with information.

"I'm afraid we don't have any good news for you. There is a back door to the City Chambers building, but it's usually kept locked."

"What's behind it?"

"An alley that leads up to the market," said Benson, "but before you ask, there is no CCTV."

"Did you check out who has keys?"

"We did," said Edwards. "The cleaning company have keys, and each of the people in the offices in case of fire."

"All of which tells us once again that our man has done his homework," offered Reilly, passing the plate round.

"He or she knew about the back door, must have known there was no CCTV and timed it all perfectly."

"I agree, Sean," said Gardener, "and sadly, none of this helps us."

As he made his statement, he overheard the voices of Dave Rawson and Colin Sharp entering the room.

"What doesn't help us?" asked Sharp.

Gardener explained.

"I'm not sure how much more we can add to that one. Dave and I paid a visit to Vera Purdy. Mainly to check on how she was."

"And?"

"Okay," said Rawson. "She is keen to see someone arrested for this, so they can all get back on with their lives. She has no idea who is behind it, but she doesn't really believe she is next."

"She doesn't?" questioned Gardener.

"No. She thinks those two were popped off because of how they were with people. She's always treated people how she found them."

"Sounds a bit naïve to me," said Reilly. "This could be someone who wants the publishing house to themselves and the only way to do that is to get rid of everyone running it now."

"Bit of a risk, though, Sean," said Gardener. "So is she eager to return to work?"

"By the sound it, yes," said Sharp. "It's all still cordoned off but she did ask when she would be allowed back in."

"Doesn't let the grass grow under her feet, does she?" said Gardener. "Which means, she could still be pulling the strings."

"She could," said Rawson, "but a search of her office didn't reveal any sets of gloves."

"Not likely to keep them there, is she?" said Reilly. "If she is responsible for this, she's one clever woman, and

167

she wouldn't be stupid enough to leave the gloves where we can find them."

"Anything on those?" Gardener asked.

"I read the company the riot act this morning. I told them I wanted the list of names by close of play today or I would obtain a warrant and seize the records myself."

"Bet that went down well."

"It had the desired effect but I haven't had anything yet."

"Go and call them, Dave," said Gardener. "Show them you mean business. *I* want those sales before close of play today, even if the close of the day is midnight."

Rawson nodded and left.

"Well I've got good news, sir," said Edwards, "even if no one else has."

"I wouldn't say that, young man," said Anderson, shouldering his way through the door, with Thornton close behind.

Gardener's mood suddenly brightened. "Why don't you two grab yourselves a drink while Patrick tells us what he's found?"

"It'll go nicely with one those," said Thornton, staring at the plate Reilly still held on to for dear life.

"And before you say anything," offered Anderson, "yes we do know the rules, and with what we have, that plate is about to disappear."

Reilly backed away into the corner. Gardener feared a fight to the death, but he also figured he knew how it would end. He turned and nodded to Edwards.

"I've finished cross-referencing all the vans in the area on the night of the Max Knowles hanging."

"And you've come up with something?"

"Yes, a VW camper van. The same van passed the area three or four times on the night in question, and finally finished up in the abbey car park."

"What time did it park up there, and what time did it leave?"

Edwards studied his notes. "From what I can see, it parked up around eleven, and left around one."

"Perfect," said Gardener, "whose is it?"

"Belongs to Adi Giles."

"Pardon?" said Gardener, as Anderson and Thornton returned.

"Adi Giles, sir. Now the problem is, it was parked well in the shadows and all I could see was the front number plate. The cameras never really picked up any activity during the hours it was parked. They only show the van as parked there."

"It's still enough to pick him up and question him. Each time we've spoken to him he has maintained that he was not out on the night, but it isn't possible for him to prove where he was because he spent the night at home alone."

"And there's been no record of his van being stolen," said Reilly.

"And his boyfriend cannot provide an alibi," said Gardener, "because he was working, but nevertheless, he needs to answer for this little event. He never told us anything about the court case with the publisher and I for one am tiring of this little boy lost act."

"How did you get on with the hypnotist?" asked Anderson, inching his way toward the plate of biscuits.

"All fine," said Gardener. "He was pretty cooperative. Said he was treating Giles for anxiety. He'd been seeing him for about three months and he felt that they were getting somewhere before Giles found Max murdered."

"And then what?" asked Thornton.

"That little episode pushed him back to square one," said Reilly, grudgingly offering Anderson a biscuit. "Apparently his anxiety is as bad as ever now."

"But something interesting did develop out of that meeting," said Gardener. "When we got there, Mantra was expecting the police because he had reported the theft of some ropes from one of his sheds."

"What does he use ropes for?" asked Sharp.

Gardener explained the phantom illusion that Mantra used in his stage shows.

"When we left the house we bumped into the gardener," said Reilly. "He didn't know anything about the theft of the ropes. Reckoned Mr Mephisto was on the bones of his arse and probably did it himself to claim the compo."

"That is interesting," said Anderson. "Has that been confirmed?"

"No," said Gardener, nodding at Edwards. "Patrick, can you go and look into that one for us, please? Have a dash around the station, find out who attended and what they know?"

Edwards nodded, closed his folder and left the room.

"Okay, Bob, Frank, what do you have?"

"We've had a good look into Polish Freddie's background," said Anderson.

"Interpol have been very helpful," added Thornton.

"Freddie has form," said Anderson, consulting his notebook. "Handling stolen goods, and a bit of GBH."

"When and where was this?" asked Gardener.

"When he was in Gdańsk," said Thornton. "He was obviously much younger then and probably got in with the wrong crowd. The stolen goods were mainly phones, and his involvement was driving the getaway van. They were soon spotted because Interpol knew about it, and they knew which van to look for, and what the swapped plates would be, so it was a no starter."

"The GBH came in when the rest of the gang all tried to fit Freddie up," said Anderson. "They all said it was all down to him. He managed to prove otherwise and they were all bailed until the police could get to the bottom of it."

"But Freddie didn't help himself," said Thornton. "While they were all out on bail he tracked them all down and gave them a serious beating. But he was caught assaulting the last one. To cut a long story short, he did about a year for it all."

"So, Freddie has a record," said Gardener. "And it looks like he specialises in an area that we would like to speak to him about. Anything since he came to the UK?"

"No," said Anderson, "he's kept his nose clean. Hasn't had so much as a parking ticket."

"But we also spoke to his boss," said Thornton. "Although he works nights, they are quite a flexible organisation, and on the nights in question, he *was* absent for a short period of time."

"Did the boss say why?" asked Reilly.

"He didn't know," said Anderson, "and to be honest we got the feeling he didn't really care. So long as Freddie did the job he was paid for, they didn't question what he did in his downtime."

"They know it's boring on the night shift," said Thornton, "and they appreciate you have to occupy your time somehow. The place isn't exactly the Ritz and I suspect a lot of stuff goes on there that the management know about. I don't think they'd appreciate us poking our noses in."

"That would all depend on what's going down," said Reilly. "If it really does connect with our case then they're out of luck."

"Okay," said Gardener, "so, Freddie has been over here ten years because his prospects in Poland fell through. When he got here the job he was after at The Ruffin wasn't available, and all they could offer was night porter. Eventually he returned and took the job, and he's been there ever since?"

"Looks like it," said Thornton.

"In all that time, he has never once tried to better himself. You know where this is going, don't you?"

"There must be something keeping him at The Ruffin?" questioned Anderson.

"Precisely, and we need to know what it is," said Gardener. "So, bring him in. Let's have him in one of the cells and let's talk to him."

As they were about to leave, Gardener stopped them.

"But before you do, grab the manager and double-check the rota, confirm he actually *was* working the nights of the murders? More importantly, see if anyone knows where he disappeared to during the short period of time he was missing."

Gardener turned to Reilly. "Does this mean that Freddie and Giles are our main suspects? Is Freddie taking an hour or two from work to sort out this mess his boyfriend has found himself in?"

"Only one way to find out, boss," said Reilly. "Let's go and get Giles as well."

# Chapter Twenty-eight

"How are you, Mrs Purdy?"

The question had come from Trevor Horn, the bespectacled sixty-year-old solicitor in the office one floor below the publishing house. He was dressed in a black suit with white shirt and black tie: portly, balding, with a sallow complexion but a comforting manner about him. Vera thought that went with the job. You very rarely found an agitated solicitor despite the amount of work they had.

He pretty much worked alone, apart from an elderly secretary in the room next door. His office was rather pristine with a highly polished desk. The carpets were deep pile and appeared to be new, but Vera knew they weren't.

He had family portraits on the wall and she knew the business had been handed down through generations.

"It's all a bit of a shock, if I'm honest."

"I'll say."

The secretary entered the office with a tray containing tea, which she placed on the desk before leaving without speaking.

"I know we didn't all see eye to eye," continued Vera, "but in my own stupid way I was rather fond of both of them. They were fighters. I didn't always agree with their policies, and I thought it could have been run better but they were in charge, so I had to bite my tongue."

"Do the police have any idea who is responsible?"

"If they do they're not letting on."

"Do you?" he asked, sipping his tea.

A phone rang in the outer office, which was quickly picked up and dealt with by the secretary.

"Not really. It's all a mystery to me. I know we have a number of court cases but nothing worth killing over."

"And you can't think of anyone yourself? You haven't had words with anyone recently?"

"Not to that extent. I've always been courteous to the people that are chasing money. I think most of them understood that the decisions were not mine."

"What does concern me, Mrs Purdy, is your safety."

"In what way?"

Horn seemed to hesitate over making his next point.

"I can't help wondering if it was just those two that have been targeted, or the business, and you know what that means."

"I know what you're saying, but who wants a business that's on its knees?"

"It may not be the business, maybe they want the office space."

"I wouldn't think so," replied Vera. "There's office space all over the city."

"But this is cheap, Mrs Purdy. People like a bargain."

"I realise that, no one more than me. But have you thought it might be much deeper than that?"

"How do you mean?" asked Horn.

"Well, your point hints towards me being next, but what if the top floor is just the start? What if someone wants the whole building? So I might be next, but who follows us?"

That comment unsettled the solicitor. "You make a good point. I hadn't thought of that."

"Did you see anyone creeping around the place on the night of Cyril's death?" Vera asked, sipping tea.

"I'm afraid not. I have spoken to the police. I was here till six thirty. When I left the only person left in the building was Zara, the designer. I checked the back door, like I always do. Stupid, really, it's just an old building with offices but I *have* become attached to it.

"In fact I've become attached to all of us. We're like a little family. May not always have seen eye to eye but we generally get on. Christmas is special. As you know, Zara always decorates her office and she puts on a little spread and drinks and we all have a little Christmas party, so to speak."

He stopped talking and appeared to be staring into space, leaving Vera to wonder what the hell he was thinking.

"So," he finally said, "like you, I can't really think of anyone who would murder any of the people in the building."

Horn glanced at his watch, which forced Vera to check hers. Time was moving on, it was after six in the evening and she wondered why he'd asked her to call round, and thought now might be the time to make mention. She didn't really want to be in the place any longer than she felt she needed to be, especially if she couldn't work.

"Is there anything in particular you wanted to talk to me about?"

"Yes, yes," he said, as if suddenly revitalised. He sipped more tea and then opened a file in front of him. "Have you had any thoughts on what you're going to do from here? I know it's a little premature but death has a way of focusing one."

Although the question had taken her by surprise, Vera *had* actually thought about it.

"Well, to be honest, I would like to continue with the business, if it's possible."

"It might be, Mrs Purdy." He organised the paperwork in the file and then continued. "I know we're getting ahead of ourselves but Max and Cyril both had their wills lodged with me."

"Oh?" said Vera. "Do you know, I never thought those two would be that organised."

"Surprisingly, they were. Obviously there is quite a lot to be sorted out and I don't think I'm speaking out of turn by having a quiet word with you now."

Vera finished her tea. "Okay." Best not to push him, she thought, don't want to appear too eager.

"In a nutshell, both wills were very similar. If anything happened to one brother, everything passed to the other. If anything happened to both, the business – such that it is – was to pass to you."

That took the wind out of Vera's sails; although she wanted the business, she wasn't expecting it. She thought she might have to fight for it, or perhaps even make an offer to take over the existing contracts and clients. That's all assuming that any of them still wanted to deal with her.

"You look a little shocked," said Horn.

"I think I am. Like I said, I never expected those two to be so on top of things. Max, maybe, but Cyril?" She shook her head. "He seemed incapable of anything."

"Well, it's something to hang on to, perhaps look forward to, Mrs Purdy. It's a nasty business all round but if you can make something of it after this then I wish you every success. As I said, there are things that need sorting, probate and the likes, but once the dust settles I think we can sign things over to you. Do you think you'll still run it from the office upstairs?"

Vera thought about that.

"Yes, I think so. It's like you said, we're a bit of a family here and I like coming into work every day and seeing all these people. I probably should have retired by now but it keeps me going."

"Good," said Horn, clearing away the files. "I'm very pleased to hear it. Now I shan't keep you any longer. Remember me to your husband, Mrs Purdy, and I wish you the very best when everything is sorted."

"Thank you," said Vera, rising and leaving Horn to finish off.

Passing through the outer office she noticed the absence of the secretary; she had either left for the night, or she was somewhere else in the building.

Vera left the solicitor's office and stood in the corridor, glancing up the stairs. What a business. She struggled to believe the events of the past week. Finding Max dead at Kirkstall Abbey was one thing, but then finding Cyril dead hanging out of his own office window was the stuff of novels.

But, like she had told the solicitor, the business kept her going, gave her something to jump out of bed for in a morning.

Vera decided she wanted to see the office. She wanted some sense of normality. Despite everything that had happened, the old building was still standing, and would continue to do so long after she had departed but she simply wanted to feel a sense of security.

She took to the stairs and wound her way up. As she came level on the landing above she could see the crime scene tape on the outside of her office door.

But something was wrong.

The last time she had seen the black and yellow tape it was in one piece, running from left to right across the door. Now, it was broken, and was left trailed on the floor. The office door was open.

Vera stood stock-still and listened but she couldn't hear anything.

Should she even be here? If she suspected something was wrong, why was she here by herself? But she could be overreacting. It may have been the cleaners. They still cleaned up as far as the landing. Maybe one of them had been nosey, or maybe they had cleaned as far as the tape and caught it.

So why was the door open?

Vera inched forward, still listening intently.

As she reached the tape, she stepped over it and gently opened the door a little further. What she saw raised the hackles on the back of her neck, caused her stomach to lurch and her legs to turn to jelly.

All Vera could do was scream. And she certainly did that. Loud enough to bring the solicitor, Trevor Horn, charging up the stairs.

Breathless, he reached the final stair and shuffled onto the landing. "Whatever's wrong?"

Vera pointed to the open door.

"Oh my good God," said Horn, reaching for his mobile.

# Chapter Twenty-nine

Gardener and Reilly were five minutes outside of Millgarth in a pool car when the call came through to Gardener's mobile.

He answered.

"Sir," said the desk sergeant, "where are you?"

"Not that far away," replied Gardener. "Traffic's heavy."

"Good, can I ask you to divert yourselves to the City Chambers, please? We have a situation."

"What kind of a situation?"

The desk sergeant explained to Gardener.

Gardener explained to Reilly.

Within ten minutes they pulled onto Kirkgate, parked the car on the pavement outside the City Market and exited. Much to the dismay of a traffic warden, Gardener flashed his warrant card so the warden put his book away.

They entered the building, took the stairs two at a time and reached the top floor to an audience of two, one of which was Vera Purdy. She stood with her back to the wall. Gardener could see the door to her office was open and the scene tape broken.

He glanced inside, surveying the scene. Adi Giles was sitting in Vera Purdy's chair. He had been tied to it with a coil of rope, which Gardener judged to be some length from the amount of coils encircling the body. He was gently rocking backwards and forwards, humming to himself. He reminded Gardener of a child. On the desk in front of him was a very large knife.

The theft of Mantra's ropes came to mind and Gardener wondered if it all fitted, but there would be plenty of time to find that out.

"Is this how you found him?" Gardener asked Vera.

"Not quite," said the man behind Gardener.

"What does that mean?" asked Reilly, staring into Vera's office.

The SIO turned. "And you are?"

"Trevor Horn. I'm the solicitor from one floor down."

Gardener nodded and tipped his hat. "Nice to meet you."

"He didn't have the rope around him when we found him," said Horn.

"Who tied him up?" Gardener asked.

"I did," replied Horn.

"Did you not think that a touch dangerous?" asked Reilly. "Especially with that bloody great knife in front of him."

"Well, we did observe him for a few minutes," said Horn. "That's exactly what he was doing when we came up here."

Vera Purdy explained why she had been visiting the solicitor. Trevor Horn said he heard her scream shortly after she'd left him. He shot up the stairs but made no move to talk to Giles at first, simply called the police. Seemingly Giles had brought the rope with him so whilst they were waiting, Trevor Horn thought it best to take the risk and tie him up in order to minimise the threat.

"But, like my partner said, Mr Horn," said Gardener, "he could have killed you."

"Had Mr Horn left him untied," said Vera, "he might have killed both of us."

"Did he resist at all?" Gardener asked Horn.

"Not at all. In fact, he didn't even seem to realise we were here."

"Has he said anything?" asked Reilly.

"No," said Vera, "just sat there humming that daft tune."

"You didn't see him enter the building?" Gardener asked.

"No," replied Vera, "like I said, we were discussing business in Mr Horn's office." She nodded toward the solicitor.

"Were you the only two in the office?"

"My secretary was in the office next door but she'd gone by the time we came out."

"Perhaps you would be kind enough to call her, Mr Horn, check to see if she saw anything," said Gardener. "And if she did, was there more than one of them? Should that be the case we'll send an officer round to take a statement."

"What about the accountant and the designer?" asked Reilly. "Are they still here?"

"I doubt Ian is," said Horn, "but Zara certainly will be."

"Just nip down and ask her, Sean."

Reilly disappeared. Gardener glanced into the outer office. Giles had not moved or tried to. He was simply staring into space, humming.

Reilly returned, confirming Zara had not seen or heard anyone.

Gardener then noticed another door on the landing.

"Where does that lead to?"

"It's a cleaning cupboard," said Vera.

"Is it locked?"

"Not usually."

Gardener strolled over and cautiously opened the door. As she'd said, it was full of mops and brushes and buckets and toilet rolls. There was little or no room to conceal yourself if you *were* hiding.

Gardener returned and glanced into Vera's office. It may have been a crime scene but he was simply going to have to enter and approach Giles, see what he could find out. All the detective had in his jacket pocket was a pair of protective gloves.

He slipped into the office, with Reilly close behind. The first thing Gardener did on approaching the desk was remove the knife and pass it to Reilly; not that Giles could have made a move for it, he was too tightly bound.

Gardener slipped around the desk, in front of the seat. "Mr Giles."

There was no reaction.

He waved his right arm in front of Giles' eyes.

There was still no reaction.

He lowered himself to the floor, checked underneath the desk, and around the legs of the chair, searching for wires, or anything that may be sending a signal to Giles; he couldn't see anything. He stood, checking Giles over for any electrical gadgets or taps; monitors in the ears. There was nothing.

Giles was dressed as flamboyantly as usual with a yellow button-down shirt, blue trousers, white jacket and the usual black beret. What Gardener did notice was a phone in the top pocket of the shirt.

Gardener glanced at Reilly. "What do you think, Sean?"

Reilly shook his head. "Looks like he's lost it. Maybe he is responsible for everything, and this has tipped him over the edge."

"Seems a bit odd," said Gardener, "that he was coming here today to possibly kill Vera, and he's just flipped before doing anything."

"It can take some people like that."

"I'll tell you what else is odd. On the night Cyril was killed, we saw two people in his office on the CCTV," said Gardener, "and with everything that's happened so far, the murders of Max and Cyril, we're certain it would have taken two people to carry them out. Why should this be any different?"

"Maybe there *was* two of them," said Reilly. "Maybe the other one's cleared off."

"Or is responsible for what's happened to *him*," said Gardener. "Leaving him to carry the can."

"Well, hopefully they've come through the front door and the CCTV across the road might tell us more."

"It's doubtful, especially if they used the back door last time."

Gardener then noticed that Cyril's office door was open, also with a broken crime scene tape. He nodded at Reilly and pointed.

Reilly stared back. "Why me?"

"Well you don't want me to get hurt, do you?"

"As opposed to me, you mean?"

"It *is* your turn," said Gardener.

"What? To get hurt?"

"Well if you remember the last major case we were on, someone stuck a syringe in me. Left me for dead."

"Damn!" cursed Reilly. "Thought you might have forgotten."

"You mean you were hoping I had."

Reilly smiled. "If there's anyone in there, he's taking the same route as Cyril. Then I'll ask questions afterwards."

"I wouldn't expect any less," said Gardener.

Reilly made for Cyril's office door. He switched on the light and stepped inside, returning about a minute later.

"All clear."

Gardener turned to Giles and addressed him again.

There was still no answer.

"Is there something wrong with him?" asked Trevor Horn.

"Or is he putting it on?" asked Vera Purdy.

"I think there's definitely something wrong with him," said Gardener. He turned to his partner. "We'll have to take him to the station, Sean. Can you call ahead, explain what's happening and ask for a doctor to be present so we can examine him?"

"I don't think we'll get much out of him."

"You're probably right," said Gardener. "But it's not just tonight I'm worried about. Judging by the way he is now, he might never speak again."

# Chapter Thirty

Later in the evening, Gardener addressed his team in the incident room.

"You may or may not all know, but we have Adrian Giles in custody at the moment and he is currently being assessed by a doctor." He went on to explain what he and his partner had found in Vera's office at the City Chambers.

"What we need to try and ascertain is whether or not he is guilty of the murders of Max and Cyril Knowles."

"Is there any doubt?" asked Frank Thornton, finishing his tea.

"In his current condition," replied Gardener, "possibly."

"What *is* his current condition?" asked Bob Anderson. "Do we know?"

"I'm afraid not. He won't talk to us," said Gardener, "or maybe he can't talk to us."

"Did he say anything at all?" asked Dave Rawson.

"No," said Reilly, "just sat there rocking backwards and forwards and humming a tune that no one knew."

"Had he been hit with something?" asked Colin Sharp.

"Not that we could see," said Gardener, "but we didn't examine him, we thought it best to leave that to the doctor."

"He's not on drugs, is he?" asked Rawson.

"Maybe," said Gardener, "but until we know what's wrong with him, I really think we ought to do what we do best, investigate the situation further."

"We might be able to help you there, boss," said Anderson. "After we met with you outside the chambers earlier, we had a root around the car parks for his camper van."

"We didn't have to look far," said Thornton. "We found it in the market's car park."

"In the car park?" asked Reilly. "How the hell did he get there in his condition? He can't have driven it himself, surely?"

"You wouldn't have thought so," said Gardener, "but we don't know that he was in that condition whilst driving the van. Whatever's happened may have done so after he left the van."

Reilly nodded.

"Well whatever happened," said Thornton, "we had the car lifted and brought back here. We had a good look round inside and we found ropes, and gloves."

More proof of his guilt, thought Gardener. But there was still something bothering him about the situation.

"Did they have Carroll's fingerprints on them?" Reilly asked.

"Yes," said Anderson. "We ran them through the system and compared them."

"So," said Gardener, "are the ropes the ones reported stolen by Mantra? Not that you can probably tell."

"Could be," said Patrick Edwards. "There's a crime scene number, but the gardener is still claiming he knows nothing about the burglary. The shed wasn't broken into, but then again, it was already open. The lock went missing some time back and was never replaced."

"You see I'm struggling with this," said Gardener. "All the way through the investigation, Giles has maintained his innocence. Even though he can't prove where he was on the night of Max's murder, he says he wasn't in Kirkstall."

"Well that's the problem, isn't it?" said Rawson. "He *needs* to prove it. How many liars have we come across that appear all sweet and innocent to start with?"

"You're right, Dave," replied Gardener. "We see our fair share of them but there's something about Giles that isn't stacking up. I just can't put my finger on it."

"We have a sighting from one of the market traders," said Paul Benson. "He did see Giles walking down the back alley toward the rear door of the City Chambers."

"Was anything mentioned about his manner?"

"Not really," replied Benson, "but then you would have thought the trader would have said something if he'd seen Giles in the condition in which you found him."

"Only if he was close enough," said Reilly.

"What's your opinion, sir?" Edwards asked Gardener.

"Not too sure, Patrick. Sean and I have investigated plenty of murderers in our time. Most of those have lied to us, but you still get that gut feeling that they *are* lying, and it's quite a challenge to prove it. But with Giles, he simply doesn't come across as a liar. I'm almost inclined to believe him when he says he didn't kill anyone."

"So who did?" asked Reilly.

"Do you think he's in league with someone?" asked Rawson. "That someone else is pulling the strings, manipulating him?"

"I think so," said Gardener, "and that brings me back round to his boyfriend, Freddie. He has form for GBH, and he has form for theft, so what else is he into? Has he slipped his boyfriend a drug, which has brought about his current state?"

"But why would he do that?" asked Sharp.

"That's what we need to find out," replied Gardener, before addressing two more of the team. "Bob, Frank, get yourselves around to The Ruffin and haul him in. It's time we spoke to him."

Gardener glanced at the girls, who had pretty much remained silent throughout the session, but to be fair he hadn't seen them all day, and they were not present at the chambers earlier.

"Sarah, Julie, we have Adrian Giles' phone. Can you go through that for me, please? Check all the numbers, the texts, the calls, and let's see who he's been talking to?"

"We're on it," said Longstaff.

"The rest of you, please keep digging into the incident tonight and see what we can find out by the morning. Meanwhile, I have asked the doctor for an assessment, and a drugs test. We also have a warrant to search Giles' house. Given that both he and Freddie will be in custody tonight we won't have a problem with that. I've arranged for a team to do that first thing in the morning. Hopefully, someone will bring us some good news."

# Chapter Thirty-one

The following afternoon, close to late evening, Gardener and Reilly stepped out of the interview room after speaking with Freddie. Grabbing a drink each, they slowly made their way to the incident room, discussing what little they had learned about him, hoping the team would have better news for them.

Upon entering, Gardener was surprised to see DCI Alan Briggs in the room. He'd obviously dropped in to see what was causing Gardener so many problems. Gardener had a quick word and then turned to the whiteboards. Following a quick update, he noticed that not all of the team were in attendance; Gates and Longstaff were missing.

Gardener explained they had had to let Freddie go pending further enquiries. They had interviewed him in the presence of a solicitor of his choice, but it had been late afternoon before *he'd* shown his face.

"Used to this game, is he, Freddie?" asked Briggs.

"He knows his way around the system," replied Reilly.

"How did you get on with him?" asked Bob Anderson. "Not very well by the sound of it."

"He didn't hide the fact that he thought Max and Cyril Knowles got what was coming to them," said Reilly.

"But he maintained it was nothing to do with him," said Gardener.

"And I take it he *could* prove this?" asked Briggs.

Gardener nodded. "We checked the hotel rota, and we spoke to his boss. He was there on both nights, and his time could be accounted for."

"Well, he would say that," said Briggs. "You know what it's like down Ruffin Street."

"That's what we thought, but until we can prove otherwise."

"If that's the case," said Frank Thornton, "what does he think about his boyfriend being the main suspect?"

"He doesn't believe it," said Gardener. "He said he's known Adrian Giles for years, he doesn't have a malicious bone in his body. He always turns the other cheek."

"I bet he does," said Rawson.

"That's enough of that, lad," said Briggs, although his expression suggested he may have found it funny.

Rawson apologised and Gardener continued.

"Freddie firmly believes that Adrian Giles is not our man."

"But if he is," added Reilly, "he's not working alone, which still leaves us with a problem."

"Freddie might still be behind it," said Anderson. "He might be controlling it all."

"But that suggests three people might be involved," said Rawson. "Freddie to dish out the orders, leaving Giles to work with, who? Of the two, you'd think Freddie was the brawn."

"The flasher?" suggested Colin Sharp.

"It's possible," said Gardener. "He certainly hasn't come forward to help us, which suggests *he* may have something further to hide."

A sudden bout of conversation from the incident room door drew Gardener's attention as Benson and Edwards came in. Benson carried drinks. Edwards had a folder with him.

"You might want to see these, sir?" said Edwards, eagerly opening the folder for his senior officer. The pair of them had been involved in the search of Adrian Giles' house.

Gardener withdrew what was inside, glancing quickly at each one. "Where did you find these?"

"In his darkroom," said Benson.

Gardener handed round the photos of Max and Cyril Knowles in their death throes. There were several of each, black and white, close-ups and long shots.

"Whereabouts?"

"There was a false tile in the floor," said Benson. "They were underneath."

"This is pretty damning evidence, wouldn't you say?" said Anderson, passing them to Briggs.

"I would," Gardener replied, "but it doesn't prove he took them or put them there. We still need to get him to talk to us, admit it, and right now that doesn't look like it will happen any time soon."

"We found something else, sir," said Edwards, passing over a box of gloves.

"Are these what I think they are?"

"The ones with Lewis Carroll's prints?" asked Gardener.

Edwards nodded.

"Yes," said Benson. "The only problem we have – in view of what you've just said about proof – is that the records do not show he bought them. We have his computer and his internet history. He doesn't appear to have been on the site."

Rawson put his arm up. "The only person to have bought them in this area lives near Ilkley, and they were delivered to a PO Box number. It was under the name Peter Stephens."

"How were they paid for?" asked Gardener.

"PayPal, according to what we have."

"In that case," said Gardener, "get onto the Post Office, see if they can shed any light at all. I doubt it but it's possible they will have details of who set up the PO Box account."

"Will do," said Rawson.

"Also, we need to find out who Peter Stephens is and what his PayPal account reveals. We might need the girls for that, they're pretty good at this stuff."

There was certainly evidence appearing, thought Gardener, but it wasn't conclusive, so it wasn't helping.

"Have we had *any* breakthrough with Giles?" asked Briggs. "Has he said anything at all?"

"No, sir," said Gardener. "We dropped in earlier and he was still sitting on the bed, rocking and humming."

"What the hell's wrong with him?" asked Briggs. "Is he going to stay like this forever?"

"I sincerely hope not," said Gardener, "but here's a man who might be able to tell us."

The police doctor appeared at the door, waving his right arm to Gardener, as if he was actually asking permission to enter. Gardener beckoned him in.

"Are you here to tell us about Adrian Giles?"

"Yes," said the doctor, a timid sounding man. He was very thin with dark hair, cut in the old-fashioned short back and sides, with a pair of wire-framed glasses. His voice was a little high pitched and he wore a double-breasted suit. "But it's not good news, I'm afraid."

"Do you know what's wrong with him?"

"I'm afraid I don't. As you know I've been with him most of the day and I can't get anything out of him. I've carried out a thorough check-up: blood pressure, pulse, oxygen levels, pretty much everything his GP would do, and I have to say he's in the best of health."

"He quite clearly isn't," said Reilly.

"But I'm afraid he is still out of it. He has not spoken a word."

"Do you have any ideas?" asked Gardener, glancing at Briggs.

"I'm afraid not, not without further tests, and for that I really need him in a hospital with a number of other consultants. If he is your man, he is definitely not fit for trial at the moment."

Gardener understood but he was frustrated. Giles was the main suspect, but they couldn't question him. If they couldn't question him, he couldn't tell them who else was involved. And without a confession, the case was going nowhere.

But where did that leave Vera Purdy: suspect or victim? Had they been in it together? Had something happened and Giles wanted rid of her? Did she beat him to it?

"I'll leave my notes with you," said the doctor. "And I'll arrange for a transfer if that's okay with you. I realise you have an ongoing investigation involving the man, but it could be some time before he speaks – if ever."

Gardener did not like the sound of the last comment, but he had no choice in the matter. He really needed Adrian Giles assessed.

"How long do you think?"

"I really couldn't say," replied the doctor. "The mind is a funny thing." As he was about to leave, he turned back to Gardener. "It's almost as if he's in a trance."

Gardener latched on to the last comment very quickly. "Pardon?"

"I said it's like he's in a trance."

"A hypnotic trance?" asked Gardener.

"That would be one way of putting it, but I'm not a specialist. You'd have to speak to a hypnotist. Do you know any?"

"Do we," said Reilly.

That pretty much silenced the room.

"Is that possible?" asked Colin Sharp. "Might he have been hypnotised in order to commit the acts?"

"Even if he has," said Briggs, "without the proof, we're stumped."

"Do you know of any cases involving hypnotism leading to murder?" Gardener asked Briggs.

Gardener could tell the DCI was thinking hard about the question.

"There are several stated cases where people have attempted to use this as a defence, but only as a defence to a charge – it'll never get them out of being nicked for the original offence. So, in this case they'd come in for murder. There has never been a case of the hypnotiser being convicted of the original offence. I've known some arrested for conspiracy, and some even convicted of that, but only on the basis that they knew and participated in the planning or execution of the offence. What are you thinking?"

"That it's a bit of a coincidence that the hypnotist treating Adrian Giles for anxiety has filed a charge of theft. Allegedly, he's had some ropes stolen from his shed."

"Has he now?" asked Briggs.

"But the gardener claims he knows nothing about it," said Reilly. "He reckoned the hypnotist probably did it himself to claim the compo."

"So we're back to square one," said Gardener. "All of this fits together nicely but there is no concrete proof."

"I wouldn't be too sure about that," said Julie Longstaff, standing with Sarah Gates inside the door to the incident room.

Gardener turned. "I wondered where you two were. Have you got something positive for us?"

"*We* think we have," said Gates.

Longstaff took over, informing the room that they had connected phone calls from the hypnotist to Adi Giles that coincided with the times of the murders.

"It is good news," said Gardener, "but it's still some way to proving the theory that we've heard."

"But why would the hypnotist be phoning Giles at the time of the murders?" asked Reilly.

"I know exactly what you're thinking, Sean, but without a recording of the phone call we're still in the dark."

Gardener turned to the girls. "It *wasn't* recorded, was it?"

"No," said Gates. "And worse still, we can also confirm that on all the occasions the calls were made, Mantra was on stage. Or was at least at the theatre."

"It would be impossible to prove he is behind all this just because he was Adi's therapist," said Briggs. "We can't convict a hypnotist on phone calls alone. We've never successfully managed it yet."

"I agree," said Longstaff. "But we can convict with solid evidence."

"What evidence?" Gardener asked.

"Better show them," said Longstaff to Gates, hardly able to contain herself.

Gates stepped over to the projector, switched it on and inserted a USB stick into it. "It appears, that fearing for his life, Cyril Knowles had a remote camera set up in his office. Everything went to his computer, which was running twenty-four seven."

"You're joking," said Reilly.

"We're not," said Gates. "The camera that recorded the information was inside a miniature Blackpool Tower on the fireplace in the office."

Gardener remembered seeing it. "You'd better show us what you have, Sarah."

Gates played the footage. The relief in the room was palpable as it showed a subdued Adi Giles and Mantra dealing with Cyril, taking him by surprise, knocking him almost unconscious, and looping the rope around his neck before throwing him through his own office window.

"Well done, girls," said Gardener. "You've played an absolute blinder. Thank you."

Gardener turned to Briggs. "We need a warrant for his arrest, sir."

"I'm on it," said Briggs, "but for now, just get in your car and get over there."

# Chapter Thirty-two

Ronnie Robinson was outside the big house on Hangingstone Lane in Ilkley. He was fuming, so much so, that he was actually shaking. But he had a score to settle, and settle it he would, *tonight.*

The house had two large bay windows either side of the front door. The one on the left was illuminated but the blinds were drawn. Left and right of the front door in an alcove were two gas mantle style lights, which were also lit. Ronnie had tried the door but it was locked.

He was pleased he'd brought a flashlight with him. He'd found it in a skip at the back of one of the charity shops in Farnley. He could never work out why people ditched stuff that actually worked.

Ronnie scurried down the path, around the side of the house. The first thing he noticed was an open shed door. He bent down a little and lurched over to the shed. It wasn't particularly big but contained a number of small gardening tools: shears, clippers, hedge trimmers. Shining the light up the sides of the wooden walls, he noticed two or three coils of rope. Ronnie took one. He may need it.

Leaving the shed, he made for the back door and tried the handle. His luck was in; it was unlocked.

He opened the door and slipped quietly inside. The kitchen was lit and Ronnie heard running water from behind another door at the back of the room, which he took to be a downstairs bathroom.

He crept forward, opening drawers, searching for something else he might be able to use as a means to protect himself. Which was a bit stupid because he's the one who would be seen as the aggressor.

But he didn't trust the bastard who lived here. Who knows what kind of stunts he could pull, or what tricks he had up his sleeve? He might even be clever enough to make Ronnie disappear without lifting a finger.

Ronnie was suddenly startled as the running water stopped. He dropped the rope behind a kitchen worktop and slipped forward towards the door. He couldn't believe his luck when he found a discarded mask on one of the counter worktops.

*Did he remove it to shower?* Well of course he did, thought Ronnie. Why would he wear it in the shower?

Ronnie slipped the mask into his pocket. We'll see how confident he is now, Ronnie thought.

But it was Ronnie's confidence that fell out of his arse when the door opened and the man he had come to see was towering above him. It was difficult to see much in the way of detail because the bathroom light was pretty powerful, which created an eerie silhouette. His hair was thick and dark but he appeared to be carrying more weight than Ronnie had given him credit for when he'd seen him the previous day.

But he couldn't see his face properly. And he wanted to; needed to.

Both men actually did a double take, which couldn't have been better timed if they had been taking orders from a film director.

"What the hell do you want?" shouted Mantra, lunging forward. "What are you doing in my house?"

"I think we both know why I'm here," said Ronnie, stepping back, wishing to Christ he *had* managed to find something in one of the kitchen drawers; and now feeling pretty stupid that he had tried to hide the rope.

Mantra suddenly stopped, and quickly glanced to his left before raising his hand to his face.

"Where's my mask?" His voice sounded like a dumper truck with a misfire.

"Ah well," said Ronnie, stepping further back, into an area of the kitchen that was better lit. "Only one of us knows the answer to that."

Mantra stepped forward, still hiding his face; but not enough that Ronnie couldn't see one of the scars, the one that lined his throat, confirming what he had suspected since yesterday.

"Have you any idea of the risk you're taking?"

"It's not half as big as the one you've been taking all these years."

Mantra slammed his free hand on the worktop, quickly retreating into the shadows. He was obviously agitated at being caught out because he started talking to himself.

"Where is it?" He opened a few of the drawers, slamming them shut when he couldn't find what he wanted. "Come on, come on."

When he finally found a spare mask, his knees nearly buckled as he opened it up and pulled it over his face. He turned quickly but didn't bother tightening the laces at the back. Obviously the fact that it was hiding his face was enough for now.

"You'd better tell me what the hell you're doing in my house before I phone the police."

"I don't think it will come to that," said Ronnie.

Mantra's body suddenly relaxed a little and his manner changed as his tone altered. "I suppose you've come to try and rescue your friend."

"My friend?" said Ronnie. "What the hell are you talking about?"

"You're too late, Mr Robinson. By now he will be in police custody on a murder charge."

"Who is?"

The expression in Mantra's eyes suddenly darkened.

"Are you that shallow that you can't remember who brought you here to try and save you?"

Ronnie's anger built quickly again. "Are you talking about Adrian? What the hell have you done with him?"

Mantra laughed, which sounded like a toy rattle. "You really are a pair of pathetic wasters. Let me tell you what really happened with your friend, shall I?"

Ronnie had no idea what he was talking about. He had come to settle a score concerning his childhood. He hadn't expected to walk into a situation with Adi. What in God's name had happened?

"He committed murder," said Mantra.

"Murder?" said Ronnie.

"Yes," replied Mantra. "He murdered those two publishers."

Ronnie's knees nearly buckled. Despite the evidence against Adi Giles being pretty damning he still couldn't accept the claim.

"You're lying. You're fucking scum, you are. You're lying, he never killed anyone."

"Oh, but he did."

"No way," shouted Ronnie. "He wouldn't hurt a fly. He's not like that. How come you're so sure it was him?"

A brief, smug smile appeared behind the mouth hole in the mask. "Because I hypnotised him, which of course, is why he has no recollection of the things he's actually done."

"Hypnotised?" repeated Ronnie, slowly beginning to lose any confidence he had, and he never had much to start with. He felt weak. "Why did you do that?"

"Because I can."

Mantra pulled out a chair and actually sat down, allowing Ronnie to see who now had the upper hand.

"Let me give you a piece of advice, Mr Robinson. If you can use someone on your way through life, do so. If you can do someone a favour, do it, but only if it benefits you."

"You're a fucking monster. Sounds like you used *him* all right, but how did it benefit you, those two being dead?"

"One would say there are many words to describe me, but the best one would be, impassive. I do things because I can, and I do not allow emotion into it."

"What did you have against the publisher? You must have had a reason, or was *that* because you could?"

"They rejected my book. They took money from me. If it hadn't been for me they wouldn't have had a business in the first place. Not only did they offend me, they have continuously ripped people off. They needed teaching a lesson."

"But why Adrian?"

"He wanted revenge, but he was too weak to do it. I gave him the strength to achieve something positive with his life."

"At what cost?"

"To me? Nothing."

Ronnie, by now, was seething inside. There had to be something he could do.

"You just don't care, do you?"

"No, of course I don't. So long as I get what I want."

"And did you? Did you actually get something out of this? It certainly wasn't your fucking book published, was it?"

"I had quite a lot of fun. Using people can be like that. It gives me a chance to prove I can do something mischievous and get away with it. But mostly, I saw those two parasites brought down."

A thought suddenly crossed Ronnie's mind. Adrian hadn't *believed* he was responsible for Max or Cyril's death, despite having photos. Knowing what Ronnie knew about both deaths, he seriously doubted that Adrian could have done it on his own. The scene at Kirkstall would have needed two people, as would Cyril's death. Until now, he couldn't work out who else could have been behind it all. It had to be the man in front of him.

But he doubted he was ever going to prove any of that. And if his friend really *was* in police custody, there would be nothing he could do right now, or ever. He had to stay focused; he had to concentrate on the reason he came here.

"I didn't know any of this, but that's not why I'm here, either."

Mantra's eyes flickered. He was suffering a moment of indecision. Ronnie had obviously thrown him.

"Well, why are you here?"

Time for the big one, thought Ronnie. He had come here for a reason and if he didn't sort it out now, he feared he would lose his nerve completely. "You don't recognise me, do you, Dad?"

Mantra flinched, and suddenly stood up from the chair. The only action Ronnie needed to see to know he had hit a raw nerve was Mantra lifting his right hand to his throat.

"Dad? What are you talking about? Who are you?"

"I'm supposed to be the stupid one," shouted Ronnie, "not you. I recognised you immediately yesterday. And don't say you didn't know who I was because you were very quick to get rid of me. You told my friend that some people couldn't be hypnotised, that you couldn't help me because I already knew my problem."

"I... I have no idea what you're talking about."

"Lying bastard," shouted Ronnie, charging across the room.

He barged into Mantra, sending him back against a worktop. The hypnotist screamed out as his back cracked against the steel, and his knees buckled.

Mantra's hand went to his face but Ronnie reached it first, ripping the mask off and launching it across the room. He pulled the man closer to him so he could observe his handy work. One scar ran from top to bottom on his right cheek, the skin puckered and drawn from the stitches that had tried to close the wound. The other was more like a hole in his throat, which was the reason his voice box didn't work properly.

"Fucking six years old, I was. You beat me on a regular basis because I never lived up to your expectations. How was that possible?" screamed Ronnie, years of pent-up frustration coming out in a torrent. "I was six, do you hear me? Six. And I was fucking dyslexic, only no one knew that, did they? They just thought I was stupid, slow to learn. How could I live up to you and your expectations and follow in your footsteps when I couldn't understand what was being put in front of me?"

Mantra tried to release himself from Ronnie's grip but he was not for letting go.

"We were in your study when you took your belt to me – again. Didn't reckon on the fountain pen, though, did you? I managed to rip your right cheek apart with the first one, didn't I?"

"Let go of me," said Mantra, still trying to break free but still failing despite being the bigger, heavier man.

"No way, sunshine. You're going to hear all of this. You made a grab for me, but I was too fast, wasn't I? Rammed the fucking thing into your throat, knackering your voice box. You needed extensive surgery.

"And after that you rather conveniently disappeared; because my mother had already died, which you probably know something about. Suspicious circumstances, they said. I'll bet they were. We were fucked, me and my sister; taken into care. That's why you wear a mask, isn't it? Not to hide your scars, but to hide your fucking shame."

Spluttering, Mantra let go of Ronnie's wrists and pushed his hands against the counter. Raising himself up slightly he stared through Ronnie and actually smiled.

"Do you find this funny?"

"I'll tell you what I find funny, Mr Robinson, shall I?"

"Go on, see if you can make my fucking sides split."

"Now you've poured your pathetic little heart out, there's not a thing you can actually do about it. There's no proof of anything we've discussed tonight. You've come here with a clear plan in mind and now we've reached this point, you really have nowhere else to go."

Ronnie's blood pressure went so high it threatened to split his head apart. He hauled Mantra to his feet and dragged him across the counter.

"We'll fucking well see about that."

# Chapter Thirty-three

Reilly pulled the pool car into the drive of the house on Hangingstone Lane. The pair of them jumped out quickly, with Dave Rawson and Colin Sharp clearing the back seats equally as fast.

Gardener walked down the path to the front door and rang the bell. As he'd expected, there was no answer. He noticed lights were on and he was pretty sure the hypnotist would be at home because he'd checked the box office at the City Varieties and he wasn't appearing there tonight.

Rawson and Sharp peered through the windows. "Can't see anything," said Sharp.

Reilly glanced through the letter box. "I can see lights, in the kitchen, maybe."

"Let's go round the back," said Gardener.

They found the back door open but the kitchen empty. Rawson and Sharp moved through the remainder of the ground floor and returned, confirming that no one appeared to be home despite the electric burning.

Gardener crossed the kitchen and checked a downstairs bathroom. A mild build-up of steam suggested it had been used recently.

"Something's not right," said Reilly. "This man is far too security conscious to leave everything open."

"Let's check outside," said Gardener.

Each man left the kitchen. Outside, Gardener noticed a large double garage further down the garden, standing off to the left. The doors were cracked open, allowing a shaft of light to creep out onto the lawn.

"Guess he's in there," said Reilly.

Gardener stepped forward, following a path that led to the building. As they drew closer, he heard a noise but he couldn't say exactly what it was.

Gardener gestured for each man to spread out and therefore reduce the angle of escape should the moment arise.

Gaining ground, further noises became apparent, a grunting sound, as if someone was straining.

Gardener sped up and ran to the door. When he opened it he was not prepared for the sight that met his eyes.

Mantra – dressed all in black, complete with mask – had his back to them, with both hands in the air, and one leg wedged against a stone block on the floor. His hands were entwined through a rope that went upwards, over a roof truss. Fighting for dear life on the other end of the rope was a much smaller man. His head was inside a hangman's noose and his hands were desperately trying to keep himself from dying, but that would never happen from the position he was in.

As Gardener threw the door further open, Reilly rushed inside pretty quickly, but he wasn't quick enough to beat Dave Rawson, who challenged the hypnotist with a perfect rugby tackle.

Both men ended up on the dusty garage floor. Colin Sharp hit the deck quite quickly, helping to secure Mantra.

Gardener pulled the rope from around the victim's neck, loosening it, and Reilly lowered him to the floor.

The man coughed and spluttered, and his face was the colour of a fire hydrant. He was breathing heavily in an effort to draw some oxygen into his lungs.

"Are you okay?" said Gardener, bending down.

The man nodded but didn't speak.

Gardener stood and approached the magician. "Would you like to tell me what this is all about?"

Mantra remained silent. He'd obviously played the game before. Gardener removed his warrant card and read him his rights; he was arresting Mantra on suspicion of murder. He asked Rawson and Sharp to take him to the station. He returned to his partner.

"Has he said anything?"

"No."

The rope victim appeared slightly calmer. He was sitting on the floor with his hands around his throat and he was almost in tears.

"Can you tell me what that was all about?"

"It was nothing."

"I see," said Reilly, "you were just helping him with a new trick, were you? Only from where I'm standing it looks like it needs ironing out a bit."

"Who *are* you?" repeated Gardener.

"Just someone trying to get justice."

"For what?" Gardener asked.

"Doesn't matter, it was a long time ago."

"It obviously does matter, son," said Reilly. "It matters enough for you to try and get yourself killed."

"Didn't though, did I?"

"Only because we intervened," said Reilly.

"And I thank you for that, but this goes no further."

"Why?" Gardener asked. "If you tell us what the problem is, maybe we can get some justice for you. After all, that is what we do."

"The fact that you're here means he's going down anyway, that'll do me."

"Can you at least tell us your name?"

The man shook his head. "No. I said what I came here to say. Once I'd done that, I never really had any idea what the hell I was going to do next."

"That much was obvious," said Reilly, "but being at the end of a rope wasn't one of them."

"Look," said Gardener, "I can't force you to tell me anything. I can't really arrest you for anything, and even though I can ask you to come down to the station, you don't have to. Even if you did, I'd have to let you go eventually. At the very least, let me call you an ambulance, you'll need to be checked out."

The man stood up. "No. No ambulance. No hospital. No names, no addresses, no nothing. You've got your man. I think we'll leave it at that."

# Chapter Thirty-four

"Nothing?" questioned Briggs.

"Not a word," said Gardener.

A little after ten thirty in the evening found Gardener and Reilly in Briggs' office. The pair were updating him on the arrest and subsequent questioning of the hypnotist.

"Any and all questions were answered by his solicitor," said Gardener.

"We didn't even get a 'no comment'," said Reilly.

"Does he think this is going to work for him?" asked Briggs. "We have him banged to rights without any admission of his guilt. Did he say why he was hanging this poor sod in his garage?"

"The solicitor reckons that his client was checking his property for the evening and he found the man in his garage trying to hang himself."

"Are you serious?" asked Briggs.

"The solicitor sounded like he was," said Reilly. "But it won't wash. Colin Sharp was quick enough to take a snap of the scene."

"Does he realise how stupid that sounds?" said Briggs. "The fact that a complete stranger would choose someone else's garage to hang himself."

"And not just anyone's garage," said Gardener, "someone who is under suspicion for murder by hanging anyway."

"And what about the victim, the man at the end of the rope?" asked Briggs. "What did he have to say?"

"He was another one who said nothing," said Reilly.

"We couldn't get anything out of him: name, address, *why* it was happening?" questioned Briggs.

Gardener shook his head. "No."

"And he just walked away?"

"We offered to call an ambulance," said Reilly, "but he wasn't having any of that, either."

Briggs didn't appear to know what to make of it. "What do you think it was about?"

"I don't know, sir," said Gardener. "When we asked him he said he was just someone trying to get justice."

"For what?"

"He wouldn't tell us that either. All he said was, it was a long time ago."

"I know it's a bit of a long shot but keep digging with this Mantra bloke, see if we can find out anything about that incident. Maybe we should try some of the hospitals as well, see if anyone admitted himself to be checked out. But don't waste a lot of time on it. It's just that, I'd like to think he was okay."

"You mean you'd like to get to the bottom of it, like us," said Reilly.

Briggs smiled and nodded. "What about this Giles bloke, has he said anything yet?"

"Not according to the doctor."

"What a strange bloody case. Nothing for ages, and when we finally pick up everyone we think is involved, nobody wants to say anything. Do they know what's wrong with him?"

"No," said Gardener. "He appears to be in perfect health and there are no traces of any drugs in his system."

"Which leads us back to an earlier theory," said Reilly.

"Go on."

"We honestly believe he's been hypnotised," said Gardener. "Mantra was seeing Giles privately to help him with his anxiety. For some reason, which we need to figure out, we believe he hypnotised Giles and coerced him into killing the publishers."

"I appreciate what you're saying but we're back to this again, aren't we?" said Briggs. "We have something here we can't prove, and even if we could, it would be the devil's own job making it stick."

"If we could get Mantra to call him and utter the magic words over the phone," offered Gardener, "maybe that will release Giles from his spell and he could talk to us."

"Problem is, boss," said Reilly, "what's he going to say? If he's been hypnotised, he won't have a clue what he's done."

"As things stand we have nothing to lose," said Briggs. "This Mantra bloke is going down anyway, but there's a lot at stake here for Giles. Why is he persecuting the man? What reason does he have for doing it?"

"But even if we manage it," said Gardener, "what's going to happen to Giles?"

"I'm not sure, Stewart. We'll have to investigate, dig up what we can, present the case, and let the courts decide. Where is this Mantra now?"

"In a cell downstairs."

"Why don't you give it a go," said Briggs, "sign his phone out, go and have a private word and see if you can get him to cooperate."

Gardener nodded and both men left the office. Fifteen minutes later, they were in the cell sitting opposite Mantra. He was dressed in prison issue clothing but he had been allowed to keep his mask on.

Gardener placed Mantra's phone on a small table between them.

"What are you doing with my phone? There's nothing incriminating on there."

"We know," said Reilly, "we've already checked."

"So what's this all about?"

"You seem to have a little more to say without your brief," said Reilly.

"I wouldn't count on it," said Mantra. "I won't admit to anything."

"I doubt that would matter very much," said Gardener, "we have enough to continue with prosecution. But we would like to ask something of you."

"Oh, we're going to scratch each other's backs, are we?"

Gardener ignored the question. "We would like you to do the moral thing here. We know you've been treating Adrian Giles for anxiety; you've admitted as much yourself. But we also personally believe that for some unknown reason you've hypnotised him and got him to do your dirty work for you."

"You two have very good imaginations," said Mantra. "You should start writing books."

"You're not the first to tell us that."

"So, you want me to call Adrian Giles. Unlock his mind and release him from his hell."

"Something like that," said Reilly.

"What, so I can help him to convict me?"

"No," said Reilly. "Cyril Knowles already did that."

There was a moment of tension within the confinement of the cell when Gardener thought Mantra was going to do the right thing.

But the hypnotist simply smiled, stood up, walked back to his bed, and left the phone untouched.

# Chapter Thirty-five

A week later, Ronnie Robinson was sitting on a bench inside the grounds of Kirkstall Abbey. It was ten o'clock in the evening, the weather had been mild for a few days, there was very little traffic around, nor any people. His alter ego probably had something to do with that.

A border collie strolled by, sniffed the leg of the bench, cocked up one leg, did its business and then finally went on its merry way.

Ronnie laughed. "Thanks, mate," he said and went back to reflecting on the last seven days.

Thinking on what the two detectives had said about being checked out, that and the fact that he found swallowing almost impossible, he had been to the hospital. They had asked all sorts of questions, and in the end he told them that he worked in construction, which took some believing considering his stature. He'd had an accident, tumbled off some scaffolding, becoming caught up in the rope. Luckily, a number of friends were on hand to help him out.

He knew the doctors were dubious about his story but they couldn't prove anything. He assured them it had been entered in the accident book and he'd been given a week off to rest. The doctor finally gave him the all-clear, to eat sensibly, and rest as advised.

His next task was to try and find out what the hell had happened to Adi Giles. The best option had been an anonymous phone call to Adi's boyfriend, Freddie, who had also asked all manner of questions that Ronnie refused to answer, before finally admitting that Adi was in St James's Hospital in Leeds.

By the time he had made that visit, Ronnie was totally deflated by his friend's condition. For the whole three hours that he was sitting with him, Adi was sitting in a chair with a blanket around his legs, staring into space. He did not speak one word.

The doctors bombarded Ronnie with questions. *What the fuck was it with these people? Why did they always want to know who you were?* Ronnie, of course, could tell them very little. He obviously knew why Adi Giles was in the condition he was in, but if he told the doctors he'd be in the next fucking room and his walls would be padded. And he wouldn't be wearing a blanket for warmth, only one jacket.

Odd that Ronnie now saw Adi Giles as a friend, considering what he had originally wanted from him. During their first phone call, and follow-up meeting, all he had wanted was to rip him off. He'd thought it a good idea to trick him into believing something that wasn't true in order to squeeze money out of him.

But that was the old Ronnie.

The new Ronnie felt that something needed to be done... or said.

Bearing that in mind, earlier today, he'd visited the police, giving a full statement of pretty much everything that had happened since he had met Adi Giles. How he himself had tried a touch of blackmail with the photos. He told them Adi had introduced him to Mantra in an effort to help with his personal problems but it hadn't worked.

Silly bastards had actually asked him about those. Like he was going to tell *them*. He wasn't wearing any of that personal question shit either; they couldn't keep him, he had called voluntarily. He hadn't committed any crime. Well, none that he wanted to admit to.

He told them about the night he had visited Mantra, once again omitting any personal data. He intimated things grew out of hand when he'd told Mantra what he knew. That was when the lunatic had attacked him and tried to hang him. Ronnie couldn't tell them he had already pinched the rope from the man's shed and what *his* intentions had been.

Finally, they let him go. Thanked him for everything he had told them, but he could see the frustration in their eyes when he still wouldn't tell them who he was.

But perhaps they knew.

"Are you okay?" said a voice, suddenly, startling him.

Ronnie turned to see a woman standing a comfortable distance away. She was mid- to late-thirties, blonde, slim, blue eyes as far as he could tell. She was dressed in a blue uniform of trousers and top. She carried a jacket over her left arm and a handbag in her right hand.

"Sorry?" Ronnie asked.

"I asked if you were okay," she said. "I wondered what you were doing, sitting out here all alone at this time of night."

Ronnie thought for a minute, before replying. "Counting my blessings, love."

"Oh dear," she said, "sounds like you've had a bad day."

"You could say that. I've certainly had better."

"And here I am sticking my nose into your affairs when all you're after is a quiet moment to yourself."

"Don't be silly," said Ronnie. "Anyway, never mind me, what are you doing out here all by yourself at..." Ronnie checked his watch "... past eleven o'clock."

She suddenly sat down, at the other end of the bench.

"My name's Caroline." She smiled. "You can probably tell what I am from the uniform."

"It is a bit of a giveaway," said Ronnie, slightly uncomfortable that a woman had suddenly struck up a conversation with him. That had never happened before. He wasn't sure how to handle it.

He suddenly smiled to himself when he thought that if she'd seen what the dog had done a few minutes previously she might not have sat down.

"I've just finished a late shift at the clinic down the road. Been vaccinating people against Covid."

"Well done, love. It's a good job there are people like you in the world; nasty business, that. Have you had yours?"

"Not yet, a bit too young."

"All the same, you're a key worker."

"All in good time. Anyway," she said, rising, "so long as you're all right. I'll leave you to your thoughts."

"I think I'm about done," said Ronnie, standing himself. "Do you live far?"

"Over there," she pointed, "about a mile."

"If I'm not being too forward, would you like me to walk you home?"

Fucking hell, thought Ronnie, he really was turning over a new leaf.

She suddenly hesitated.

The new Ronnie pressed on. "I'd rather that than read about you being attacked by the flasher in the paper."

"When you put it like that." She smiled. "Anyway, with you around, I don't think the flasher will try anything."

"No," said Ronnie, "I don't think he will."

"Better put these on," she said, holding up a mask.

Ronnie laughed. She should have seen the one he was wearing a couple of weeks ago.

\* \* \*

Gardener and Reilly were finishing up in the incident room. They had a folder, and a number of other piles of paper in front of them, as well as a drink each. They were discussing the unknown man's testimony that had been made earlier in the day. They were pleased that he had been checked out at the hospital, and that he had finally come in to make a statement; but not so pleased that he continued to remain anonymous.

"I've been thinking about that," said Reilly.

"Go on," said Gardener, taking a sip of his tea.

"I have a feeling I know who he is."

Gardener glanced at his partner and smiled. "You think he's the Farnley Flasher, don't you?"

"So do you," said Reilly, laughing. He stood up. "I reckon we've been working together far too long."

Gardener laughed with his friend. "Maybe," he finally said, "but I wouldn't have it any other way."

If you enjoyed this book, please let others know by leaving a quick review on Amazon. Also, if you spot anything untoward in the paperback, get in touch. We strive for the best quality and appreciate reader feedback.

editor@thebookfolks.com


www.thebookfolks.com

# ALSO AVAILABLE

*If you enjoyed IMPASSIVE, check out the other books in the series:*

## IMPURITY – *Book 1*

A seasonal worker is killed using a lethal drug unknown to forensics. Another Santa is next in line. Can DI Gardener stop this festive spree, or is the killer saving his biggest murderous gift till last?

## IMPERFECTION – *Book 2*

When theatre-goers are treated to the gruesome spectacle of an actor's lifeless body hanging on the stage, DI Stewart Gardener is called in to investigate. Is the killer still in the audience? A lockdown is set in motion but it is soon apparent that the murderer is able to come and go unnoticed. Identifying and capturing the culprit will mean establishing the motive for their crimes, but perhaps not before more victims meet their fate.

## IMPLANT – *Book 3*

A small Yorkshire town is beset by a series of cruel murders. The victims are tortured in bizarre ways. The killer leaves a message with each crime – a playing card from an obscure board game. DI Gardener launches a manhunt but it will only be by figuring out the murderer's motive that they can bring him to justice.

## IMPRESSION – *Book 4*

Police are stumped by the case of a missing five-year-old girl until her photograph turns up under the body of a murdered woman. It is the first lead they have and is quickly followed by the discovery of another body connected to the case. Can DI Stewart Gardener find the connection between the individuals before the abducted child becomes another statistic?

## IMPOSITION – *Book 5*

When a woman's battered body is reported to police by her husband, it looks like a bungled robbery. But the investigation begins to turn up disturbing links with past crimes. They are dealing with a killer who is expert at concealing his identity. Will they get to him before a vigilante set on revenge?

## IMPOSTURE – *Book 6*

When a hit and run claims the lives of two people, DI Gardener begins to realize it was not a random incident. But when he begins to track down the elusive suspects he discovers that a vigilante is getting to them first. Can the detective work out the mystery before more lives are lost?

## IMPIOUS – *Book 8*

It could be detectives Gardener and Reilly's most disturbing case yet when a body with head, limbs and torso assembled from different victims is discovered. Alongside this grotesque being is a cryptic message and a chess piece. A killer wants to take the cops on a journey. And force their hand.

## IMPLICATION – *Book 9*

When a body is found in a burned out car, DI Stewart Gardener quickly establishes that a murder has been concealed. But with a missing person case and a spate of robberies occupying the force, he will struggle to identify the victim. When the investigations overlap, he'll have to work out which of the suspects is implicated in which crime.

## IMPUNITY – *Book 10*

After a young woman passes out and dies, the medical examiner makes a grim discovery. Someone had surgically removed her kidneys. Detective Stewart Gardener must find a killer evil enough to think of such a cruel act, let alone have the gall to carry it out. It looks like revenge is a motive, but what had the victim, by all accounts a kind and friendly girl, done to anyone?

## IMPALED – *Book 11*

When Gardener is called to investigate a crime, he has no idea of the terrible scene that awaits him. The corpse of a man has been found with nails driven into his chest and no hands. There are no witnesses to the crime, just reports of a strangely dressed man seen nearby. Gardener feels a serial killer is at work, and the clock is ticking.

*All FREE with Kindle Unlimited and available in paperback.*

www.thebookfolks.com

Printed in Great Britain
by Amazon